TWO BROTHERS

GOOD VS EVIL

GEORGE M. GOODWIN

For information contact: info@palehorsepublications.com
Cover Art by Michael Thomas
Cover design by Pale Horse Publications
Edited by Sharon L. Harris
Published by Pale Horse Publications
November 2021
10987654321

They had the wagon loaded with all of the things that they would be able to carry with them on their trip to the west. At least everything that they could do without at the time. The cook stove would have to wait until they were ready to leave, if in fact that time came. The table and chairs would be left behind to save space, Pa had made them himself. Another one could be built when they arrived. When what was a true necessity had been loaded and room left for the younger boys to sit, Pa managed to get only a few of Ma's things that she had from her mother on there. She had a large set of dishes her mother had brought all the way from England. Pa explained to her that they would probably get broken in the wagon ride. Ma agreed and she took them to town and sold them to the store owner. There was two things Pa and Ma had been good at in this last twenty-six years together, raising crops and raising children. Ma and Pa had been born not two miles apart, in the hills of Tennessee just outside of Chattanooga. Even as kids growing up, they always knew they were meant to be together. At fifteen, Pa had bargained for four acres of land by clearing some ten acres of land.

Then, cutting and hauling enough trees for a cabin for an older man who could no longer do the hard heavy work himself. When he was finished with that, he set about and built a cabin of his own on his own four acres. Then, on the very day he finished it, he walked that two miles to ask for Ma's hand. Her father had seen the kind of man Pa was to become.

Knowing that his daughter would be well taken care of, he had said yes. Three days later at church, after regular service was over, they were married. Every day, Pa worked that land from daylight until after dark. Digging and burning out stumps and rocks, he cleared two full acres for planting. Every year it produced enough to keep them eating vegetables all year and even some little bit to sell. Although he didn't know it in the beginning, he soon would have plenty of help. Pa was also a good hunter, so he and ma lived a pretty good life. Every year or two, another child was born. Ma, who had been born Sara Renee Marsh, was a big reader of the bible and so, as the boys came along, they were each given names that she had read from it. Samuel was their first child, born in 1835. Isaac came a year and a half later, in 1837. Almost exactly a year later the twins, Daniel and David, were born in 1838. Then, Michael came next in 1840, Jacob in 1841, Josiah in 1843 and then Abraham in 1844. Eight children and not a girl in the bunch. Pa, was born Benjamin Franklin Blackstone in 1818.

He was twenty-six years old when Abraham, the youngest, was born. He told Ma it looked like there was to be no girls for them and they decided that eight children was enough anyway.

He told Ma, "I know the good book says, 'go forth and multiply', Ma, but he wasn't talking to just us. Let some of those others folks help out a little."

Pa was a studying man, not so much of books, although he could read and write, but more a studier of men and the world around him. He talked very little but listened a lot. He saw a change coming to this country and maybe it was needed, but he had a feeling that a war was coming with it. This war, though, would be different than the one his grandfather had fought in. That one was fought against the British for independence and it was clear who the enemy was. This one would pit neighbor against neighbor, brother against brother, and father against son. It was a war Pa wasn't sure this young country could recover from. If so he thought, it would take many years.

Between the planting he done and the game his sons brought in, they were living as easy as anyone in the hills and easier than most. In 1860, while in Chattanooga, one day he heard some men talking, saying that some of the southern states were considering seceding from the union if Abraham Lincoln won the presidency in the fall. It wasn't just Tennessee, he said, it was several of the other states as well. This country was about to tear itself apart over slavery.

Slavery, yes, but also the way they felt about other things as well. They believed that in most things, the individual states should govern themselves without

Washington and the federal government becoming involved. Talk was that, if elected, Lincoln had plans of freeing the slaves. Pa had never and would never own any slaves. He held no desire to hold any person in servitude against their will, no matter what their skin color. There were, however, a large number of people who owned slaves. The big plantations in the Carolinas, in Georgia, Mississippi and Alabama would not be able to grow their massive crops of cotton, rice and tobacco without them to work the fields. They were the ones it would hit the hardest, but there were a lot of others who agreed with them. Not that they did or wanted to own slaves, but they wanted the choice to be their own and not the federal government, with each state governing itself in the matter of slavery.

Many said their forefathers had not fought for independence from England's rule to live under another ruler. Their idea was that Washington should take care of politics and deals with foreign countries, but that each state should govern itself. Pa and Ma talked about it and decided they would have their things packed and ready should Lincoln win. Pa was sure it wouldn't be long after that. Ma said she would give none of her sons to fight in a war over something she felt both sides carried wrong in.

Lincoln won the election on November sixth and, on the eighteenth day of that month, Ma and Pa Blackstone and all their boys headed west to Texas. A neighbor told

Pa he thought it cowardly of him to go. Pa's first thought had been to hit him right in the mouth. Instead, he just told him to see if he felt the same way when his sons were dead from fighting a war that didn't truly even affect him.

"I will be somewhere in the west, happily living with my wife and my children," said Pa.

From outside the city of Chattanooga, they went due west as well as the roads would allow. They weren't really roads at all; often just used trails that had been used for years. They finished the first leg of their trip to Memphis in twenty-four days. It was the twelfth of December when they pulled into town. Talk there was that South Carolina had officially seceded from the union and that a group of secessionist had attacked Fort Sumter already.

"And so it begins," Pa told them.

Pa talked to several different men and found out what they thought would be his best route west to Texas. It was far different than it would have been on horses. From Memphis, they traveled to Little Rock, Arkansas. They arrived there on December the twenty-third. Groups of men were gathered here and there, talking of war, and Pa decided it would be best to just get what supplies they needed while they were still available and somewhat affordable and to travel on a ways.

Ten miles outside of town, Pa stopped the wagon at a likely spot near a small stream and they stayed camped there through Christmas Day. Back at home, Christmas had always been a big time with them, decorating a tree and making gifts for one another. They would miss that this year, but it could not be helped, and at least they were all together. Very soon, a lot of families would not be.

"The war is coming," said Pa, "and I just hope we are beyond its limits when it starts."

The next leg of their trip would be the longest part of it. He was headed to Fort Worth in Texas, still some three hundred sixty miles away. Even with the supplies they had bought in Little Rock and some still they'd brought from home, the boys had to hunt every day. It took quite a lot to keep ten people fed. That was no problem, though, because all of the boys could hunt. They had been taught to shoot a rifle from the time they were as tall as that rifle. Not much later, they learned to shoot with pistols as well. Other than the team, they had only four horses for the boys to ride, so as they rode along, four would walk and hunt close to the path of the wagon and four would hunt farther out. It was slow going with the wagon. On a good day, they may make twenty miles, but then on a bad day it would be closer to ten. Two days short of a month, on the twenty-second day of January 1861, they came into Fort Worth. Word there was that five more states had seceded.

Texas, so far, was not one of them and neither was Tennessee, but from the talk Pa heard, everyone thought they soon would be. He had hoped when they left Tennessee that Texas would be as far as they would have to go. It seemed now maybe not, but they would move on to Abilene and see how things were there.

They came into Abilene eleven days later with a wheel about ready to give out and a tired bunch of horses. By now, back east, a full scale war was getting ready to start. Both sides were getting troops in position. They learned there that Texas had seceded from the union the day before they had arrived. There was also talk that Lincoln was calling for troops to move south to suppress the rebellion. If armed soldiers moved southward, they would be met by resistance. So far, Tennessee still had not seceded.

Soldiers were gathering in Abilene getting ready to go east. Some of them wore grey uniforms, but others were still in their homespun clothes. Both sides were getting their troops in position and men were heading east from every town it seemed. With the last of their money, Pa had gotten the wheel worked on, but the man made no guarantee as to how long it would last. Once again, they moved on, but not very far. About forty miles out of town, the wheel gave out completely, dropping the back of the wagon to the ground with a jolt.

Pa looked at the wheel, then at the boys, and said, "This is where the Lord has decided we stop. If they bring their war this far, then we will defend ourselves. We will protect what is ours against all who come, no matter the color of their uniform."

With a little looking around, they found that the place they had come to could not have been any better picked. All around them were low rolling hills with waist high brown grass blowing in a gentle wind. There was a good sized creek there with some mighty sweet water in it. By its size, Pa figured it to run all year. In places, the creek had spread out into large pools or ponds. Also, they had saw no sign of any other people living within ten miles of them. Here, they had land enough to raise stock if they wanted to.

Ma thought here they had room for her sons to marry and build their own cabins. Back in the hills a few people had raised hogs, but Pa himself had never been partial to keeping them. They were usually owned by families that had no shooters in them and no other way to get meat. Pa had no shortage of that, but told them to build shelters first.

"When that is done, start hunting."

February on the plains was no colder than mid-fall had been back in the hills, so game would still be plentiful. The boys blocked up the back of the wagon level at the bad wheel. Pa and Ma would shelter in there. The boys quickly built shelters big enough to sleep two. They had been doing this all their lives, so it went quickly. They were nothing more than a frame, open at both ends, but made to keep out the dew or rain.

Pa pulled up a hand full of the tall brown grass and looked at the soil clinging to the roots. He had grown a good garden back in the hills and the soil here looked to be a lot better than what he'd had back there. He was a good farmer and with this soil he thought he could do very well. As soon as the shelters were finished, the boys took up their rifles and went to hunting. Spring would be here soon and Pa knew that the boys would bring in more meat than the family could use. Maybe they could take some into town and sell it to raise money needed for seed before spring.

That evening was no disappointment for him. Between the eight of them, the boys brought in three antelope and a white tail deer. One of them brought in some kind of small wild pig. Although Pa had never seen one, he knew it was pork when he saw it. The other boys brought in about a dozen sage hens and two of the biggest hares Pa had ever seen. Jacob also told him that there was fish a plenty in at least one of the ponds.

The weather was fair, so the boys slept well in their open end shelters. That night, Pa decided to ride out tomorrow himself and look at what trees there were close by to be used for a cabin. They would start it soon enough, but other things needed to come first.

On the third day they were there, Pa went with Jacob to the pond and, even though the other boys did well on their hunt, that day they had fresh fish for supper.

Everyone thought it a nice change. Every night after supper Samuel would read to them from the bible. All of the children could read and write; Ma would have it no other way. She, herself, had been taught by her mother who had been a flatland schoolteacher. That was, until her pa had wooed her away to the mountains. Samuel, though, seemed to not just read from the bible, but to really enjoy reading from it and to have a better understanding of it than they did.

When they had a good supply of dried meat and smoked fish, Pa made up two big bundles and tied them to one of the team horses. They were a matched pair and he would ride the other one. He would take the jerky and fish into town and sell it. He left early in the morning for the two hour ride into town, telling the boys and Ma that he should be back before dark. The boys went hunting soon after pa left. When they came in that, he still wasn't back. Michael wanted to go and see if he'd had trouble.

"We will give him a little longer," Ma told them. At six o'clock, he still wasn't back, so Isaac, Michael and Jacob saddled up and headed toward Abilene. Samuel was against it, saying Pa had not told them to do so.

"No," said Michael, "but he did say he would be back before dark and he's not. Clearly he has had some kind of problem, Samuel."

About ten miles out from camp, they met Pa coming toward them walking. As they drew up, Michael noticed that Pa looked disheveled. More so than just from the walking he'd been forced to do. Jacob climbed down and got Pa up on his horse and Jacob climbed up behind him.

"What happened, Pa?" Michael asked him. "Where are the horses and what happened to you?"

"It was nothing, Michael," pa told him. "Let's just go home, okay?"

"Pa," Michael insisted, "where are the reds?"

Pa knew that Michael was very partial to the big red horses. Pa had bought them as colts and Michael had been the one to feed and raise them. Now, Pa had watched all of his sons shoot all their lives and all of them were good shots. For Michael, though, a pistol was like a part of his hand. Not only could he get the gun out and into action very fast, but rarely missed what he shot at. He was also the only one of his boys who had a temper to speak of. He didn't want to tell Michael, but he finally gave in.

"Some soldiers took them from me," said pa. 'A group of them were about to ride out as I rode into town this morning and they were short of horses."

"And the meat?" asked Michael.

Dropping his eyes to the ground, Pa said, "They took it, too.'

"What time was this?" he asked his father.

"Around eight this morning," Pa said.

"I'm going after them," said Michael.

"No," Pa said. "Just let it go, Michael."

"Like hell I will," he said, and turned his horse and charged off in the direction of town. When he reached Abilene, he went first to the marshal's office.

"How can I help you?" the marshal asked Michael.

"My father had his horses stolen. There was also two large bundles of dried meat that he intended to sell this morning. They were stolen this morning by some soldiers."

"They weren't stolen," said the marshal. "They were seized by the confederate soldiers as they were needed for the war effort."

"It's not my war," said Michael. "The horses and the meat, however, were and I will have them both back."

"What you need to do, son," the marshal said, "is to go home and let things alone."

"What you need to do," Michael told him, "is get some guts or a different job."

The marshal made a move for his gun, but before he even reached the butt with his fingertips, Michael held his in his hand and pointed right at the marshal's chest.

"Ease it out slowly and toss it away," Michael told him. When the marshal had done as he was told, Michael said, "My father was also beaten."

"He wasn't beaten," said the marshal. "They just roughed him up a little because he didn't want to let them have the horses."

"You mean the horses that our family depend on and the meat that all of us have hunted and skinned and dried? You saw this happen and you did nothing?" said Michael.

'What could I do?" he said. "They're the army."

"I will give to you what the other men gave to my pa," Michael told him. "Then, when I catch them, I will give them what horse thieves get, or worse, if it is their choice."

"What do you mean?" asked the marshal.

"Horse stealing is punishable by hanging," said Michael, 'but if they are not in the mood to be hanged, I will shoot them."

He holstered his gun and hit the marshal in the mouth in one fluid motion. He saw right away that this was not truly a man in front of him, but a coward hiding behind a badge. He hit the marshal twice more and left him lying in a heap with the suggestion that he seek other employment and walked out.

Back at the family's camp, everyone was still up when Pa and the boys rode in. They started asking questions about what had happened and where was Michael. Pa told them the same story he had told Michael and the others out on the trail. Ma brought him a plate of food, knowing that he'd not eaten all day.

"Michael went after them?" asked Samuel.

"I tried to stop him, Samuel," said Pa, "but you know your brother and his temper."

"God help them,' said Samuel, "for they have started a war before they even reach the east. This one, I'm afraid, they have no chance of winning."

When he finished eating, Pa said, "Let us all go to bed. It is late and we have things to do in the morning."

"What about Michael?" asked David.

"We will trust him to God," said Samuel. "Now, go to bed like pa said."

The boys went to their shelters and Pa and Ma to the wagon. Once inside, she said, "Ben, are you okay really?"

"I'm fine," said Pa. "Just a little sore. It may be I'm getting old," he said. "But then, you know I was never much of a fighter even as a youngster back in the hills, Ma."

"You are worried about Michael?" she asked him.

"I am worried about those soldiers," he said. "There were only ten."

Now, Ma had also watched them grow up and she was proud of the fact that all of her sons could shoot and shoot well, but she had never seen anyone as fast with a pistol as Michael was. She favored none of her children over the others, but Michael had always seemed to be the one to come to their rescue when needed. She knew he would go hard on the men who had laid their hands on his pa and she was happy with that.

Michael rode through the night, and when he found their camp in the morning, he checked the ashes of their fire and knew he was only an hour or two behind them. He put two pieces of jerked antelope meat in his mouth, took a drink from his canteen and mounted up again. They had stopped at noon to let the horses rest and to catch a nap themselves. Michael quietly rode up on them and caught them all napping. He walked his horse over to where one of them was propped against a tree. His rifle lay across his saddle horn and the strap of rawhide that held his pistol in its holster while riding had been removed.

"Howdy boys," he said loudly, and they all jumped like they had woke up in an ant bed. "Where you boys headed?" he asked them. "Y'all headed to the war in the east?"

"You looking to join up one of them?" asked Michael.

"Haven't made up my mind yet," he said. "Say, those are some fine looking animals you got over there."

"That one you're on don't look so bad either," said the man.

"Who belongs to them two big red ones?" Michael asked.

Two of the men, who hadn't spoke before, did now.

"They belong to us," said one of them, as the two of them stepped into the clear.

"Had them long?" Michael asked.

"Raised them from colts," said the man. "Me and my brother here did."

Michael looked at him and said, "Mister, you are a liar."

"Boy, that kind of talk can get you killed around here," said one them.

"So can stealing horses," Michael told him.

"What are you saying, boy? You saying we stole them horses?"

"Well, it took you a minute to whittle down to it, but I think you finally got the point," said Michael. Now, these boys seen that his pistol was on his right hip, so they assumed he was right-handed. His rifle barrel was pointed at them, but the trigger of it was a way over to his left side and away from his right hand.

"Son, I think I'm going to have to kill you," said the one who had been talking.

"It's your party," said Michael. "You call the dance."

The two who had claimed the horses both went for their guns. Neither of them made it; one took it right in the chest and the other through the throat. Both hit the ground, dead. Michael's left hand was on the rifle trigger. At that range with a rifle there was no need to even check them boys. As he shot them, he'd also drew his pistol with his right hand to cover the others.

"The music's already playing," said Michael. "Any of you other boys want to dance. As he swung his rifle their way, he saw sixteen hands reaching for the sky.

"Mister, we had no part in it," said the first one he had talked to. "We only met them in Abilene and they wanted to ride east with us. Thing was, though, they had no horses. We told them we would give them until yesterday morning to get some or we were riding out without them."

"Did you see what was done?" Michael asked him.

"No," he said, "but we heard about it later after we had left town. They showed up with horses so we left."

"Did he give you part of the jerked meat?" Michael asked.

"Yes, he did," said the man.

"Get it out," Michael said, "all of you. I'm taking it and the two horses with me."

"We won't make it to Fort Worth without that jerky," said the man.

"That, sir, is your problem, not mine," he told them. "Besides, if you boys can't shoot well enough to feed yourselves, a war is the last thing you need to be in."

Most of the jerked meat was still there and, with a rifle aimed at them, they were very helpful in packing it on one of the big red horses.

"Now get," said Michael, "before I decide to shoot you all."

"Shouldn't we bury them?" the man asked Michael.

"You bury men," he said, "not horse stealing skunks. The coyotes will take care of them, now get."

Two days later, Michael rode into their own camp. Pa was the first to reach him.

"Are you okay, son?" he asked him.

"I'm fine, Pa, and I brought back your horses. I also stopped through town and sold the meat." Reaching in his pocket, he handed his father fourteen dollars. "The man at the store said he'd buy all we could bring him."

Samuel walked up as Pa took the money from him.

"Michael," he said, "I see you got the horses back."

"I did," he told Samuel.

"Did they just give them back and say they were sorry?" he asked Michael.

"No, they weren't very nice guys," he said. "But we knew that already from two of them beating on Pa, didn't we, Samuel?"

"How many, Michael? How many did you kill?"

"Only the two who hit my father and stole his property," he told Samuel. "I was in a good mood so I let the others go."

"That gun of yours will bring you to grief, Michael," said Samuel. "It will bring trouble to us all."

"If trouble comes, Samuel, I will handle it."

"The Bible says 'thou shall not kill,' Michael."

"You're right, Samuel, but I believe it also says 'thou shall not steal.' Maybe if them guys had met you first, they'd still be alive." Michael walked away from them and went to his shelter.

"Pa," Samuel said, "he cannot right all wrongs in life with a gun."

"Nor can you with a bible," said Pa. "I heard you praying last night, Samuel. You asked God to send our horses back. You didn't say how, though," Pa said, and then he walked away, too.

Pa went to speak with Ma about what had taken place. "I know it is not right to kill, Mother, but if Michael had not done this, we would be short two horses and our money for seed. I fear there will be trouble between Samuel and Michael, though. They are brothers, but they are men also and have very different ways of looking at things."

"I will think on it," said Ma.

The other boys were glad to see the horses back when they came in from hunting. Those two horses were very important, not just to pull the wagon, but in working the fields and helping with the dragging of logs. They could do the work alone that it would take two of the riding ponies to do.

That evening, Pa had them take the plow out of the wagon and all of the farming implements. After supper that night, Samuel said he did not feel like reading.

"Then we will talk and plan," said Pa. "Tomorrow, I will start plowing the land for growing. It is more than I can do alone, so in fairness, until it is done, half of you will hunt and the other half will work with me. The next day, you will switch jobs and so on. Does everyone agree with this?" Pa asked them. Each one raised their hands. This was how Pa had always done things with his boys.

The next morning, Pa sent the oldest four to hunt. This had been Ma's suggestion to keep Samuel and Michael apart until their tempers cooled. The second day, he sent the four youngest to hunt. The third day, the two oldest and two youngest, then repeated the first day over.

The separation worked, as most of Ma's ideas did, and soon Samuel and Michael were talking as normal again.

When the workday was over, Michael had taken to riding into town sometimes. Pa happened to be awake very early one morning when he rode back into camp. He smelled of alcohol and tobacco and walked drunkenly toward his shelter. Pa decided now wasn't the time to talk to him about it.

He had found out many years ago that he had little patience for a fool or a drunk. The drunk, however, would eventually sober up. There was little hope for the other one. Maybe he wasn't a normal Tennessee mountain boy, but Pa had tried drinking only once in his life. He found that it was not for him. *"There were other ways than fussing to stop this,"* he thought. They had finished with the plowing, so that same morning, Pa sent half to hunt and the other half to falling trees he had marked for the cabin. Michael would be in that group today. If he felt like going into town after falling trees all day, it would be a big surprise to Pa.

During Samuel's bible reading that night, Michael had a hard time holding his eyes open. As soon as Samuel was through, Michael went to his shelter and was soon sleeping. The next day, Pa switched them up and let Michael go hunting. At supper that evening, Pa named the ones that would be on trees tomorrow. Knowing he would be falling trees again tomorrow, Michael decided to stay at home again that night.

They now had another good surplus of jerked meat and smoked fish. Pa would ride into town the following day to sell it and with that, and the fourteen dollars Michael had brought back to him, he would buy seed. They were also in need of a few supplies Ma needed like salt and meal. They needed coffee as well, with every one of them drinking it.

Everyone would have a day off and the twins would ride into town with Pa. Pa chose them because they were more even tempered than Michael, but were probably close to as good with guns, if it was needed. He also wanted to remove the temptation of having a drink from Michael for a while longer. Michael surprised him by picking up a fishing pole and heading to the pond. Josiah and Abraham followed suite. Michael had said nothing to anyone about what he'd done to the marshal. The fact was, he had thought no more about it since the night he rode after the horses.

So, Pa got an ear full from the owner of the general store about it. "Thanks to that boy of yours, we don't have a marshal any longer."

"You never did have one," Pa told him. "All you had was a prop for a badge. He stood right there on the porch of his office and let those two men knock me around something awful. Then, they stole my horses and other property. If you need a marshal that bad, maybe one of my boys would be interested," said Pa.

"Not the one that came that night," said the store owner.

"No," said Pa, "that one doesn't have the temperament for the job or for people who can't do for themselves, but I have seven others. If no one in town wants it, I'll talk to them and see if they might. But they are grown men and make their own decisions."

When he had the seed and other supplies gathered up, Pa paid him and left. He said nothing to the twins about the job. He would wait until after supper to tell all the boys at the same time about the marshal's job being open.

"I didn't know if any of you would be interested, but I told the man at the store I'd ask."

"What happened to the one they had?" asked Jacob. "Did he get killed?"

"No," said Pa, "he wasn't killed, just advised to seek other employment for his health."

"You mean somebody run him out of town, don't you?" said Josiah.

Smiling, Pa said, "Yes, son, that's what I mean. Isaac, I thought you might be their best choice. With you being the oldest, other than Samuel, it is your right to decide."

"I don't know, Pa," said Isaac, "but I'll ride in tomorrow and find out more about, it if it's okay with you."

"It's fine with me," said Pa.

Michael sat by the fire after the others had all turned in for the night. When he was sure they were all asleep, he said, "Sorry I didn't tell you about that, Pa. It just slipped my mind as I didn't think it that important."

"Well, I felt quiet sure they wouldn't want you for the job, Michael. That's why I didn't suggest it earlier."

"Pa, that man stood and watched two men half your age beat and rob you. I couldn't let him go with that."

"Michael, I appreciate your thinking of me, but, son, you walk a fine line between doing right and doing wrong. Just go a little easier with your temper or one day you may slip into being what you think now that you are against."

"I will, Pa, and again, I'm sorry about not telling you."

"Okay, son, get some sleep tomorrow we're going to start dragging the logs here for the cabin."

The next day, they all worked at the logs, with some dragging and some trimming limbs. They were soon all at the site. It was a long day, but by supper, they had most of it done. Isaac had come home earlier and told them that he would be taking the marshal's job. It would pay him thirty dollars a month and meals, but he would have to live in town and sleep in the back of the marshal's office. He would be the first one of the boys to move away from the family.

That night, Ma cooked his favorite meal. She also did some sewing and patching that was needed on his clothes. Ma being Ma, she couldn't let him go to town with shabby and torn clothing. None of the other boys had much to say about it. Isaac was the quiet one of the bunch, but he was always there to help with the work and always done his part, or more. Even though he was sometimes a little too bossy to suit them, he would definitely be missed.

For the next week, the boys all worked hard in raising the cabin. By the end of the week, though, Ma and Pa were ready to move in. The inside wasn't finished, but that was something Pa would do himself. Later, they would all build better shelters for themselves. For now, though, they were fine with what they had.

So, Isaac became the first one of them to take an outside job. The people of Abilene really took a liking to him. He kept fights at the saloons to a minimum and was happy to help anyone with any kind of problem. A town marshal there to help the people. He rarely got rough with the rowdies, but once they saw that he could.

Samuel took to riding into town on Sunday morning to attend church. Sometimes, some of the others would go with him, although, Michael was never one. The twins, David and Daniel, were the first ones to build a real cabin for themselves. It was hard to separate those two when it came to anything. Ma always said she hoped when they were ready to marry, they found two women who got along, for everyone's sake.

When shelters were better built and the crops were planted, it didn't take all of the boys to keep them in meat. The older boys started to take the horses and go wandering. They were just getting to know where they were, so to speak. They had done the same thing back in the mountains. Samuel cared nothing for the exploring and was often the only one of the boys in camp all day. Sometimes spending whole days reading the bible.

In May, the twins came back from San Angelo with news that Virginia, Arkansas and North Carolina had seceded. Tennessee still hadn't, but was putting their own troops together and were expected to at any time. They also brought back word that they would be taking the marshal and deputy jobs there. Seemed theirs had joined up to go east and fight in the war.

"We'll still come to help with the fields at harvest time, Pa," they both told him.

"If not," said Pa, "there are others who have no jobs yet."

It was nearly eighty miles to San Angelo and Pa couldn't expect them to come often.

Michael rode out often, too, but Pa had a feeling he wasn't going to church and wouldn't be coming home with a badge. The last Saturday in May, Isaac rode out to visit. He told them that Michael had killed a man in town.

A saloon fight over a card game on Friday. All who had saw it said it was a fair fight, so he was not in trouble, but Isaac had asked him to leave town.

"Was it a soldier?" Pa asked him.

"No sir," said Isaac, "it was a gambler who showed up a few days ago. I was about to run him out of town myself, as I'd heard complaints from other people that he was a card cheat."

Pa told him about David and Daniel taking jobs in San Angelo. Samuel had walked up while they were talking about Michael having killed the gambler. He said nothing, but Pa could tell he was very upset with Michael. Some hours after Isaac rode back to town, Michael rode in to the cabin.

"Isaac tells us you have killed another man," said Samuel, before Michael had even got his horse unsaddled.

"Yes, Samuel, I did. He was cheating at cards and I called him on it," said Michael. "He reached for his gun and I beat him."

"If you had not been drinking and playing cards in the first place, you would not have been cheated," Samuel said.

"Well, I guess you've got a point there, Sam, but I was and he did and now he won't do it anymore."

"You're a disgrace to Ma and Pa," Samuel said to him.

"Go easy, big brother," Michael told him. "You may push too far with your religion."

"Why don't you just leave, Michael, and quit embarrassing our parents?"

"That's enough, Samuel," said Pa. "This is your brother's home just like it is yours. If anyone is going to tell anyone to leave, that will be my job and my decision."

Samuel turned and walked away.

"Sorry, Pa," said Michael, "but sometimes his religious piety gets to me."

"As I'm sure your lifestyle and beliefs get to him, too," said Pa.

The Tuesday after their altercation, Samuel came to the cabin of his parents and ask to speak with them.

"Of course, son, come on in," said Ma and Pa together. He told them that he had been ask to preach at the church in Abilene. There were times when the traveling preacher couldn't make it so they had asked Samuel to preach there full time.

"At first, I was not going to take it," he told them, "but perhaps it would be best for me to not be here all the time."

"Is this about you and Michael?" Pa asked him.

"It is, Pa," said Samuel. "I cannot let the trouble between Michael and I come to trouble between you and I. Pa, you know what he does is not right, but I understand why you say nothing to him. You and Mother have always let us find our own way. I'm just sorry that he has chosen the wrong way."

"You are a good son, Samuel," said Pa, "and a good man also, but you must learn that you are not your brother's keeper. I, too, hope that Michael will find the right way, but it is I choice he must make for himself. If you or I try to hound him into it, he will simply ride away."

"Well, anyway, there are some small living quarters on the back of the church," said Samuel. "I will be living there."

In June, Tennessee seceded. Missouri and Kentucky did not secede, but they sided with and helped the confederacy is any way they could. Three days after Samuel left for town, Michael rode in with a wagon behind him.

"What are you doing with a wagon, Michael?" Pa asked.

"I brought it to you," he said. "I bought it from a man in town. It should help at harvest time. It's old, but seems in good shape."

"Where did you get the money to buy it?" Pa asked.

"Okay, Pa, I won it playing poker and I know how you feel about cards, but I knew no other way to get it for you. I did no cheating; it was won honestly."

"Thank you, Michael," said Pa, "for your honesty and for the wagon. It will be a great help because I believe we will have a good harvest."

"Pa, did Samuel leave because of me?" Michael asked him.

"No," said Pa. "Your brother has gone on his own accord. He has taken the church in Abilene." "

I'm sorry he is gone, Pa. I feel like it is my fault."

"It isn't the fault of either of you," said Pa, "it's just a difference of opinions and lifestyles. Of course, that is really all this war is about, too, if you look at it."

"If all four of them are gone, then you are short of horses here," said Michael.

"We have the reds," said Pa, "and there is less hunting required with so many gone. Besides, Samuel will be bringing his horse back, as they will provide one for him and a carriage as well."

Michael stayed for supper with them, but it seemed the younger brothers were leaning more toward Samuel's way of looking at things. Even Jacob, who had been his shelter mate since they were children, upon first seeing the wagon, asked Michael if he had stolen it.

The next three years saw Jacob take a job as marshal in the town of Comanche. It was a small town some one hundred and twenty miles from the farm. It also saw Isaac get married and the confederacy start to lose the war, for the most part. Michael had visited the farm very little in those years, often staying away for months at a time. They often heard of some killing he was involved in and later even robberies. Pa refused to believe the robberies at all and said, of the shooting, he was sure they were fair fights. They heard stories of him being as far away as Kansas and even down in Mexico.

On January 31st , 1865, congress passed the 13th amendment abolishing slavery. On the ninth of April 1865, the war was declared over when General Robert E. Lee surrendered to General Ulysses S. Grant at Appomattox Virginia. On April 15th, President Abraham Lincoln was assassinated while attending the theater with his wife. None of this meant very much to Pa. He was sorry Lincoln had lost his life, but for a man that Pa thought mainly responsible for the deaths of so many others, he truly thought justice had been served.

In June of that year, though, Ma died. She had gotten a cough back in the winter and it just never went away. Pa felt like his whole world fell apart. All of her boys were there when she was laid to rest, except for Michael. Samuel, who had moved to Fort Worth and was preaching there, came, but could not give the sermon for his mother saying it was just too painful.

Two days after Sara Blackstone was laid to rest, Samuel went back to Fort Worth. Josiah and Abraham, who were the only two left at home, went with him to seek jobs as peace officers there or in nearby towns. Abraham became town marshal there in Fort Worth and Josiah found the same position in the town of Waco, Texas.

The night after they left, Pa sat alone in the cabin. Alone for the first time in thirty-one years. A light knock at the door brought Michael into the cabin. He crossed the room and hugged his father.

"Pa, I tried to get here, but I was in Mexico and could not make it in time. I am so sorry."

"It's okay, Michael. Your mother always knew you loved her and she also knew that you traveled great distances at times. She would hold no anger toward you, son. She was proud of all her sons."

He and Pa sat long over coffee that night and talked of what Michael didn't know about his brothers. "Michael," said Pa, "you are my son the same as your brothers and I have never took their side over yours, but I have to ask you why."

"Why what, Pa," asked Michael.

"The way you live," said Pa. "When it was only talk and gossip, I paid it no attention. Now, though, I have seen with my own eyes the wanted posters from other towns, and even other states, that hang in your brothers' offices. Wanted for murder and for robberies of stages and banks. I do not ask you to be like them, for I raised you all to be true to yourself, but as a father, I have to know one thing, would you ever raise a gun to your brothers?"

"I would not, Pa, you have my word on that," said Michael. "I honestly don't think I would be able to. I know, also, that even though we don't agree on many things, they would never raise one to me. I keep away from the towns where they work so that they are not put in that position."

"Now you will add two more towns to that list," said Pa. "Your brothers, Josiah and Abraham, have gone to Fort Worth to seek peace officer jobs as the others."

"I will learn where they find it and stay away as with the others," said Michael. "What of you, Pa, what will you do here alone? You can't farm all of this by yourself."

"No, I can't do that, Michael, but I can still hunt for myself and grow a garden to supply what I need. I miss all of you being here, but as a father, I am also proud that I raised capable men."

"Even me, Pa?" asked Michael.

"Yes, Michael, even you," said Pa. "I do not agree with the things you do and I worry about you, but it is your life to live. I lived mine the way I chose. Even the move west was my way of saying I'd let no other choose for me what he thought best."

Michael was gone even before Pa awoke in the morning. *"A man with a price on his head couldn't afford to stay in one place to long or he may stay there forever,"* Michael thought to himself. He rode west when he left the cabin, avoiding the town of Abilene altogether.

Michael was in Amarillo when the marshal there recognized him from a wanted poster and came to the saloon to arrest him. As he stepped in the door with his gun drawn, he said in a loud voice, "Michael Blackstone! I am here to arrest you."

"I have done no wrong in your town," said Michael.

"You have in others and I shall hold you for them."

"You're a town marshal," said Michael. "Just take care of town business, that is your job."

The marshal said again, "Michael Blackstone, you are under arrest, now stand up."

He sat looking at a three king and a pair of deuces hand that he hated to fold. "Gentlemen," he said to the men playing with him, "one of you just got lucky. I fold." As he threw his cards on the table, he drew and fired before the marshal knew what was happening. As he walked past the marshal's body lying on the floor with a crimson spot staining the front of his white shirt, the man who'd sat beside him in the poker game turned over his cards.

"Three kings and a pair of twos," he told the others.

A posse gave chase for some miles, but a few well-placed shots soon made them ask themselves just how much they'd really liked the marshal any way.

Three weeks and one stage holdup later, he was in Dallas. With the war over, Yankee soldiers were suddenly everywhere, it seemed. It was something he would just have to get used to, he guessed. After all, they did win the war. Michael did try to watch himself, but that same night in the saloon, he ran into one of them blue boys who just pushed and pushed again.

When Michael won his third hand in a row, the soldier said, "You sure are one lucky cowboy."

Michael let it go as just joking. The next one, he threw in what would have been the winning hand. He hoped to avoid any more jokes. When he won two more in a row, the Yankee soldier said "cheat" under his breath, but clearly could be heard by all at the table. Michael let that one go as poor upbringing.

When he won the next hand, which was dealt by the soldier himself, the soldier slammed down his cards and said, "Nobody is that damn lucky."

Now, back in New York or somewhere, he might get away with that, but the trouble was, he was in Texas and he'd just called Michael a cheater. "Mister, I'll give you just three seconds to take it back and then I'm going to kill you."

"Said it and I meant it," said the soldier.

Michael was the last man in Texas he'd ever say it to. That big hole in his forehead would make sure of that. As he stood up from the table, Michael's first thought was if there were any more soldiers in there. Scanning the room, he saw none, so he picked up his winnings and walked out.

There were no soldiers in there, but there was a face that he had not recognized, but that person sure knew him. No more was Michael out of sight than the man stood and walked out, too. It took him a minute to find the others, but then he told them that one of their own had just been killed by a wanted man.

"How do you know he's wanted?" they asked him.

"The marshal's office has papers on him and I knew him from when I was a marshal out in Abilene," he said.

When Michael left the saloon, he did what he always did. He asked for his room key at the hotel desk, went upstairs to his room, locked the door, put the key on the bedside table and went out the window. That empty hotel room had saved his life more than once. From there he went to the livery stable. He saddled his horse and then lay down on the hay to get some sleep. It sounded like half the union army firing and, peeking out the front door, he could see the stabs of flame in the upper floor of the hotel where his room had been.

"I think it's time to go," he said to his horse, as he climbed on. Killing the oil lamp hanging near the front door, he opened it just enough to get out and around the side of the building. By the time them soldiers thought to look in the stable, he had been on the trail for almost twenty minutes and a man on the move can make a lot of distance in that amount of time. Not that any of them were anxious to follow him into the dark anyway.

"That was two towns and two killings. Maybe it was time to visit Pa," thought Michael. *"First, though, a trip over to New Orleans to do some gambling."* He was hoping to make a little more in Dallas, but now that was out of the question.

Things went better in New Orleans. In two nights of cards, Michael picked up over six hundred dollars. He liked having money in his pocket and that was strange because he had not grown up that way. Cash money was something you hardly ever saw in the Tennessee Hills. If you couldn't grow it, make it or shoot it back there, you swapped what you could grow, make or kill for it or you lived without it. His first rifle he had swapped a big white tail buck for it. He'd killed the deer with Pa's rifle.

Michael had meant what he told his father and he avoided any town where one of his brothers was a marshal. Right about now, though, he was none too happy about having so many brothers. He knew there were wanted posters on him and he didn't want to take the chance that someone in their towns would recognize him and then they would be obligated to arrest him. He meant it, too, when he said he'd raise no gun against any of his brothers. He held no animosity toward them for being lawmen. Like Pa said, he'd raised them all to be whatever they wanted to be. In New Orleans, he'd noticed a lot of people left displaced by the war headed west. A lot of them wouldn't care how they made their living as long as they made one.

His brothers were about to have their hands full enough, he thought. Michael edged his way around Dallas as he rode back west. For the short period of time he had been gone, it would still be too hot with soldiers looking for him.

His fourth morning at Pa's cabin, he looked out to see at least two dozen soldiers riding toward the farm. He ducked out the door and around to the corral. Pa was there with his horse already saddled.

"I'm sorry, Pa," he said. "Somebody in Dallas must have known who I was."

"Ride, Michael," said Pa. "I will tell them I've not seen you for months."

As Michael rode away, he kept the cabin between the soldiers and his back. "I think this may be a good time for us to check out California," he said to his horse.

As he rode away that day, he never thought it would be almost six years before he would see his Pa again. Towns were few and far between; it was mostly broken desert and strange shaped mountains that he rode through. There were small bands of Indians everywhere. He had known quite a few Cherokee and some Choctaw Indians back in the hills of Tennessee, but these tribes were unknown to him. Twice he got into running battles with them, but had come out lucky both times.

Thirty-six days after leaving the farm, Michael rode into Phoenix, Arizona. Phoenix was wide open as far as he could see. No soldiers in town, just a lot of folks drinking and gambling and having a good time. He had never been here before, so he didn't fear being known.

It was his kind of town. It had been a hard trip, so Michael checked in at the hotel. In his room, he bathed from a basin of water and shaved in what passed as a mirror. He dusted his clothes and hat, wiped his boots and checked his pistol, then went to the first saloon he saw. It took him only a minute to find a seat in a poker game. By the fourth hand, Michael had lost over half of his money. As the fifth hand was dealt, he saw the dealer work the cards. He was not nearly so good at it as he thought he was and, if Michael had not been so tired, he would have seen it sooner. Michael let the hand play on until it was only he and the dealer left in. It was the dealer's raise and he did so. Michael called and laid down his hand, a full house jacks over threes.

When the dealer laid down four kings, Michael called him for a cheating skunk. The gambler across the table from him said, "I'll give you that one, boy, as just being too dumb to know better, if you get up and walk away right now."

"Can't," said Michael, even louder. "I named you for a cheater and that's what I meant."

The gambler reached for his gun, but Michael shot him twice in the chest, knocking him over backward in his chair. As the dealer hit the floor, one of the other men who was playing at their table said, "Look there. Two cards; a two of diamonds and a four of spades had fallen from his coat sleeve. You're right," he told Michael, "he was cheating."

Just then, somebody toward the back of the saloon yelled out. As the crowd looked around, a man setting at a table there slumped forward, shot in the back. The man was setting directly behind the dealer. Michael was sure both of his shots had hit the dealer. They had, in fact, but one had went right through the dealer and into the other man. It was a pure accident, but suddenly, the sheriff was there and Michael was in handcuffs.

The man at the other table was a local business owner. He was also a well-liked man to make matters worse. Three days later, Michael stood before the judge, also a local man and longtime friend of the man killed in the saloon. The judge heard the story of what had happened from the sheriff. The other card players told their version also, saying that when Michael had called the dealer a cheater, the dealer had went for his gun and Michael had beaten him. They also told how after the dealer hit the floor, they saw the cards fall from his coat sleeve. The judge shuffled some papers on his bench and looked down at them. The sheriff had brought him several posters on Michael from towns in Texas. There was also one from the U. S. Military for the questionable death of a soldier in Dallas. Maybe it was a fair shooting and maybe not. Michael had not stayed around to clear himself, so he was presumed guilty.

Looking at Michael, the judge instructed him to rise. As Michael stood there the judge said, "Michael Blackstone, in this court, on this sixth day of April 1868, as a duly appointed judge for Phoenix, Arizona, you stand before me, charged with two counts of murder. I have heard the witnesses and I am ready to rule. As to the charge of murder for the unnamed card dealer, it is my judgment that you are innocent as he drew first, making it self-defense."

Michael knew he was about to be released. The other man had been an accident, pure and simple.

"As to the charge of murder by reckless behavior to Ned Miller, a local businessman, husband and father who was shot in the back, I find you guilty and I sentence you to five years at hard labor."

As the sheriff led Michael away, the deputy asked the judge, "Why such a harsh sentence? It was clearly an accident."

The judge handed him the stack of wanted posters. "Because I could not sentence him for these," he said.

Michael began his sentence right there in Phoenix. For six months, he worked twelve hour days making mud brick for the first post office to be built in Phoenix. In October, he was moved to San Quentin State prison, located north of San Francisco in California, to serve out his remaining time. On the trip there, a guard and another prisoner were wounded when a band of Indians attacked their wagon. Michael helped the remaining guard fight them off and then helped him tend the wounded and get on to the prison. It turned out the wounded guard he'd helped save was a nephew of the warden.

The other guard told how Michael had helped him fight off the Indians and then helped make it on to the prison, at a time when his own escape might have been possible. The warden showed leniency in Michael's hard labor sentence. He only worked outside two days a week and the rest in the kitchen or the sick ward. To a Tennessee boy who had slept outside most of his life and worked with an axe felling trees regularly, or sometimes moving huge rocks from fields, being confined to the inside was far worse than those two days swinging a pick or hammer.

The warden did it out of kindness, though, and Michael never said a word. He never wrote to any of his family to let them know where he was or if he even still lived. All but his father would have thought he deserved what he got anyway. He just did his time quietly, making no trouble for the guards or anyone else.

On the fourth day of April 1873, the same guard who he had helped with the Indians years ago as he was taken to San Quentin, came to Michael's cell and opened the door. "Michael," he said, "the warden wants to see you."

In the warden's office, he was told that his sentence had been served and he was free. Warden Daniels handed him the clothes and boots that he had worn the day he came there and then, from his own pocket, he handed Michael a twenty dollar gold piece. "Take this," he told Michael, "and leave California. Go home, if you have one. If not, go anywhere, but I have seen too many released from here be right back within a few months if they stayed around."

Michael bought a ten dollar horse from an old Mexican man. The horse wore no brand at all, so he could hardly be accused of stealing it. Before leaving San Francisco, he spent six dollars for a used rifle and four on coffee, rifle shells and tobacco. That was something he had picked up a taste for while in prison. No one in the family ever smoked.

He climbed on the horse and headed for Texas. On the ride to Texas, Michael wondered if his father was still alive. He also wondered about his brothers. He rode to the farm and saw the cabin that he had helped his brothers build. A steady smoke rose from the chimney, so he knew someone was there. A knock on the door and Michael heard a familiar voice say, "come in."

He opened the door and his father stood facing away from him at the stove. "Hello, Pa," he said.

The older man almost dropped the pan he held. "Michael," he said, before turning around.

"Yes, Pa, it's me," said Michael.

His father turned and came to him, wrapping him in a bear hug. "I told them you weren't dead," said Pa. "I told them all." His father asked if he had eaten and Michael told him not for two days.

"I will put on more food," said his father, "and some coffee as well."

Over coffee, Michael told his story of where he had been for almost six years.

"You have changed," Pa said. "You've grown older. Of course, we both have, but you talk different, too. You seem more calm."

"What of my brothers?" Michael asked him. "Are they all well?"

"Yes," said Pa. "Samuel is in Dallas. He started his own church there some five years ago. I have been told it is the largest church in Texas now. I have not made the trip to see it myself."

"What about the others?" asked Michael.

"They are all Texas Rangers now, Michael," said Pa. "Daniel and David joined two years ago, when it was still being called the Texas State Police, helping with recovering from the war. In May of this year, though, the Texas legislature appropriated seventy-five thousand dollars to be used to organize six companies of seventy-five men each to clean the outlaws and bandits and renegade Indians out of Texas. They are very powerful, Michael."

"Are you saying I should leave again, Pa?" Michael asked him.

"You know I would not tell you to leave, Michael. I only meant that, without your brothers, there are still many others. The boys have promised me they would never raise a gun to you, but there will be a lot of other rangers who will."

"Maybe I will go to Mexico," said Michael.

"You know," said Pa, "many people thought you were dead these last years, Michael, why not use that to start over with your life? I don't mean you should be a preacher or a peace officer, but you could stay here with me and we can farm again. If you'd like, we could even try ranching some. Maybe a few cows or horses. What do you say, son? Will you think about it at least?"

"I will, Pa," said Michael. "I will think about it."

He stayed in the cabin with Pa that night, as none of the shelters had been kept up since the last of the boys had left home. The next day, Michael started to work to remake his shelter and was working on it when they rode in. Isaac and Josiah walked out to where he was working on the shelter.

"Hello, Michael," said Isaac.

Looking up from his work, he said, "Hello, Isaac, hello Josiah. Good to see you boys."

"What are you doing here?" asked Isaac.

"Rebuilding my shelter," said Michael. "The cabin was built for just Ma and Pa."

"No, I mean what are you doing back here in Texas?" said Isaac.

"What do you mean?" said Michael. "It's my home."

"No," said Josiah, "it was and could have been from now on, but you made the choice to leave it. Go back to where you have been these last six years, why don't you?" said Isaac.

"Go to hell," Michael told him. Isaac made a move as if to reach for his gun. "Don't," said Michael. "I promised Pa I'd not raise a gun to any of you boys, Isaac, but if you try it, I will have to kill you."

"You think you're still that fast, Michael? I'm sure they didn't let you practice in prison."

Something in Michael broke and he said, "So, you knew I was in prison."

"Yes," said Isaac, "we all knew. Well, all but Pa anyway."

"The soldiers that came for you the day you left said you killed a soldier in Dallas over a poker game," said Josiah. "Is that true?"

"No," said Michael, "not over a poker game. I killed him because he called me a cheater and then went for his gun."

"Whatever your reason was, you caught a lot of attention when you did it. Him being a member of the Army made it a crime against the government. They threatened to put Pa in jail for covering for you until we convinced them that you hadn't been around here for some time and that Pa wasn't lying."

"How did they know who I was even?" asked Michael.

"Do you remember the marshal in Abilene that you beat when Pa was robbed before the war started?" asked Josiah.

"Yes, I remember him," said Michael.

"Well, he was in the saloon that night and sent them straight here."

"What about Phoenix?" Michael asked them. "Did you know when I was arrested there and why?"

"Yes," said Isaac. "The sheriff there sent out wires trying to get information on you. You see, he said that the gambler you killed there was a fair shooting, but your recklessness caused another man's death, too. In most cases, it would be considered an accident. However, if other peace officers had had problems with you, it would be taken into account by the judge."

"So, all of you sent him posters on me from Texas. Is that what you, mean Isaac?"

"Yes, Michael, that's exactly what I mean," he said. "All of us tried for years to tell you the road you were headed down, but you wouldn't listen. Samuel left home because of your actions and the embarrassment it caused him. I will admit, you stayed out of the towns where we were marshals. Every other town was fair game to you, though."

"Why was I told none of this at the time?" came a voice from behind them.

Jerking around, Isaac said, "Pa, I didn't know you were there."

"Obviously not," said Pa, "or you would not have said what you did. Is it true, Isaac, and you, too, Josiah? You helped to put your brother in prison for an accident? Then lied to me for all these years and tried to convince me he was dead?"

"No, Pa," said Isaac. "It was for what he'd done around here, too."

"He was not on trial for that, Isaac," said Pa, louder than Isaac could ever remember hearing his father in his life.

"We thought it would do him some good," Isaac told his father.

"Do a man good to be caged like an animal for a crime he had not committed?" asked Pa. "I have always been proud of you all. I didn't agree with the way Michael was living, that is true enough. I want you to remember, though, that if that so-called marshal in town had done the job he was hired for, Michael would not have had to. Instead, he hid behind it with his false righteousness. I see the very same thing here. Maybe there was reason for Michael to do what he done, because the man who should have didn't. Do not hide behind that badge, Isaac."

"Do not take my side, Pa," said Michael, "please. I know what I've done is not right."

"Neither is plotting and planning behind a badge with others doing the same. I told you one time years ago. Michael. to be careful or you would become what you were against. I say that to the two of you now," he said, looking at Isaac and Josiah. "You cannot uphold the law by bending it to fit your personal beliefs. Isaac, you said it was your opinion that sending Michael to prison would do him some good, change him from the way he was living is that your thoughts."

"Yes, Pa, it is," said Isaac.

"Then why is it you came here and told him this was not his home? That he needed to leave here and even to leave Texas? You have not seen your brother for six years. How do you know it didn't help him? How do you know he hasn't changed? You gave him no time to prove if he had changed or not. You work for the state of Texas, but, Isaac, you do not own it. No, Isaac, this is my home, and at least until you and your brothers look at your own wrongdoings, I wish for you to leave and you, too, Josiah."

Isaac started to reply, but his father turned his back on them and walked away. When they had gone, Michael went into the cabin. "Are you okay, Pa?" he asked.

"I'm okay," he said. "Michael, I'm sorry."

"You're sorry? What are you sorry for, Pa?"

"All of this," he said. "If I had stood up for myself that day in town, maybe you wouldn't have had to."

"None of that was your fault, Pa," said Michael. "Like you said out there, that marshal should have done his job. I have done other things, though, Pa. I have killed no man in doing so, but I have robbed stages and once even helped in a bank robbery. I have stolen no horse from no man though. Maybe Isaac is right in wanting me gone, Pa. I'm not like them you know. I think I will go to Mexico, for a while at least."

"Maybe you should at that," said Pa. "Not because they are right, but I thought for a minute out there today that Isaac was going to draw on you."

"I know," said Michael. "I saw it, too, and that's why I think it may be best. Today Isaac, tomorrow maybe one of the others. Especially now that they are Texas Rangers."

They both sat in silence for a moment. Pa said, "Michael, he wouldn't have made it, you know. I know, Michael. I have known for many years. None of your brothers would have a chance against you, maybe even no two of them."

Michael rode out two days later. Pa would not let him leave on the plug horse he'd bought in California, though. He made Michael take one of the big red horses and even a bill of sale for it. He also gave Michael a fifty dollar gold piece. Pa said, "Michael, I have a rifle I can shoot game enough to keep me eating you keep your money. It will be enough to buy you a game somewhere."

When he rode out that day, they both knew it was probably the last time they would see each other. Neither would show it though.

Bandits And Rangers

Michael had avoided the towns where his brothers were marshals out of respect. Now, they were rangers, which meant all of Texas was their job. He left Texas and went to Mexico, but they had pushed too hard this time. He was forced out of Tennessee because of a war that he did not want either side in, and now he was being forced out of his own country. Well, it was something they would come to regret, this he swore to himself, as he rode away from all he knew as home.

Michael had been down in Mexico several times before and knew some people who lived in Juarez very well. In less than a month, Michael had four men riding with him on raids over into Texas. Abilene was his first stop in a string of many. They rode in one at a time not to draw attention to themselves. Michael was the last to come in and he went straight to the bank.

The bank president met him halfway of the large room and said, "Unless you are here to do some business for your father, we don't need or want your kind in here."

He was Michael's first shot, but not to kill; he was shot in the shoulder. When he fired that shot, every eye in there went to him. Two men reached for their guns but would never get the chance to do it again. Some of them had headed for the door, only to find that two men stood there blocking any escape. Their pistols were drawn and they were blocking the doorway.

As Michael dragged the wounded president to the safe, outside, the marshal had heard the shots and was headed to the bank. He had been the marshal there for less than a year and now the town would need another one. He had only the thought of stopping a bank robbery in his mind and not of the robbers themselves. He saw them too late and went down in a hail of bullets from the bandits.

With the safe opened, Michael took all the paper money in there and shoved it in a sack. He knew none belonged to his Pa, as he would never put money in a bank. Then, he took what gold there was and put it in a different sack. As he neared the door, he knocked the president out with his gun butt. He turned toward the people standing big eyed at the counter, and said, "Y'all brought this war on yourselves."

They were back in Mexico before a wire even reached anyone who could help them. Once they were across the border, they slowed down and relaxed. That night, they camped near Juarez. They counted the cash and split it five ways right there. The gold Michael held onto to hide away for later. There may come a time when it would be much more needed than now.

A week later, they hit Forth Worth in much the same way. The marshal was killed, as was one citizen and one of Michael's own. Quickly, they darted back across the border and into Mexico. This time, the robbery drew the attention of the Texas Rangers. The Ranger who was sent there listened to the description of the bandits by the witnesses, but Jacob had no idea that one of them was his own brother.

Michael had always been dark, but living in Mexico, he had grown even darker in complexion and had grown a small mustache and goatee. He was thought to be just another Mexican bandit. Michael and his men rode now toward New Laredo. There, he recruited two more bandits and they rested and spent most of their money they had taken in Fort Worth. He knew the Rangers could not cross the border to get them, so they had no worry of that.

A month later, they rode from New Laredo all the way to Waco. The take there was small and his boys were disappointed, so before going south again, they hit the bank in Austin as well. The money there was considerably more and they fled back across the border. Michael would not tell them so, but he knew Waco would be small pickings. But, he hit it for another reason of his own. They were happy with the take in Austin so all was well.

After a week of drinking and laying around, they once again rode north to Juarez. Michael was sure that his band's next robberies would get the attention of some, if not all, of the rangers. Right now, it still appeared to be just random robberies by Mexican bandits. He would hit Comanche and San Angelo next.

That would tell his brothers it was him. At least if they were any kind of lawmen, it would. The towns he would have hit, save for Austin, was the ones where his brothers had marshaled and kept him from going to them out of respect for all those years. That was all over now. Once he was through with those two towns, he would rob and steal from anywhere he decided to.

Pa had removed them all from being in the war back in Tennessee. They were going to be in one now, though, he would see to it. Before that, though, Michael had to make a ride by himself. Leaving the others in Juarez drinking and womanizing, he rode toward the home of his father all alone. It was the first time Michael had been back in almost two years.

He came to the farm in the early morning hours. There was no smoke from the chimney. That was unusual, as his Pa had always been an early riser. Michael rode up to the cabin and climbed down from the big red horse. A knock to the door brought no answer. Another, harder one, got the same response. He lifted the latch and walked inside, calling his father as he did so. Pa wasn't there and had not been there in some time, he thought. No one had been, for the air in there was stale. Walking out, he went next to the barn. Nothing; no horses, no Pa, just quiet.

A stab of fear went through Michael and he started toward the cottonwood tree. It was a huge and lonely old tree out by the creek. Dread filled every step he made until he reached the spot. There before him was not one, but two headstones. Standing before them, he read again his mother's, which he had done on many other occasions. Then his eyes went to the other one. Benjamin Franklin Blackstone, it read, born 1818, died 1876. Beloved husband and father. May he rest in peace. Pa was gone then, for some months it appeared, maybe even more. He must have died shortly after Michael had rode away the last time.

Michael stood there with tear-filled eyes, and said, "I'm sorry for all the grief I brought to you, Pa. I never done it on purpose. I guess there's just something wrong with me."

Michael did not go back in the cabin, but just mounted up and rode away. Now, Michael knew that none of his brothers ever really knew where he was, but word of his father's death could have reached him on the outlaw trail just by talking of it in saloons. It was this way that he had learned of his mother's death, and at that time, he was also in Mexico. That meant that they had deliberately kept it from him like it was none of his business.

"Okay, Rangers," Michael said to himself, *"I'll show you what is my business."* It was over now. He had sworn to his father he would never raise a gun to any of his brothers and he would stand by that. That said, though,

there were men he rode with that was not their brother. He rode as straight as possible back to Juarez. By the time he arrived, the boys were broke and sober, so as soon as he rested, they would leave.

They would head for Comanche and San Angelo. When he left their towns, it would be broke and some of its citizens would be bloody.

"Now we will see if you are any good at your job, boys."

There were now ten in Michael's band of outlaws and they hit Comanche like a cyclone. When they rode out, the bank, the saloon and even the general store had been robbed. Eleven men were dead and their telegraph wires were cut on either end of town, preventing them from wiring for help before Michael was through in San Angelo.

San Angelo was next, and they showed no mercy there either. They happened to catch their bank holding a rather large gold shipment, probably headed somewhere back east, thought Michael. In all, they loaded their horses and stole four more from the livery stable to pack away the gold. The livery owner would not be needing them anymore. Twenty people lay dead or wounded when they rode out.

They headed for the border, and this time, they would ride all the way to Chihuahua before stopping for more than overnight. In Chihuahua, with the flash of a gold, they were treated like kings. Food and drink of any kind, women, horses and clothes fancier than anything Michael could ever have imagined. They were too flashy for the lot of them, and besides, they wanted to not be seen. Michael's top man, known only as Valdez, had a cousin living there who was not a bandit, but for a little money, he would be a spy for them.

While the cousin made his way into Texas to listen and get what information he might on what the Rangers were doing, Michael and his band just rested. He would give it some time to see if his brothers were so very smart as they thought. They had plenty of money for now, so they had no need to make a raid right away.

Michael met a woman there and spent much of his time with her. He was waiting for the spy to return. Two months from the time he left, Valdez's cousin returned. He came straight to Michael.

"They know it is you, Senor," he told Michael. "By the towns you targeted, yes, but mostly from people who remembered that big red horse of yours. The Rangers they set and wonder where you will strike now. The ones with a last name as yours say they do not know where, only who. Senor, I learn, too, that the gold you took in San Angelo was headed to Austin to be the payroll of all the Rangers."

"Well, now they're working for free," said Michael. "Let's find out if they will work as hard."

"They are thinking, Senor, that you will go to Abilene or that area. I think the ones with your name are telling them this."

He paid the cousin well for the information and told him he would be needed again. Michael called the boys together to plan their next hit.

"The Rangers seem to believe we will hit again in Abilene next," Michael told them. "While they concentrate on Abilene, we will give them a big surprise and run them around for a while. We are ten now, so my plan is that we divide into two bands. One group will ride from Juarez and hit the town of Lubbock and then Brownsville on their way back. The others will ride from Acuna to raid Houston and the small town of San Antonio. We will meet back in Acuna and ride together to Chihuahua. These Rangers will not expect us in two places so far apart, you see."

They planned their raids to hit when least expected. They were all well-armed with the best weapons available. They all rode good horses, tested and true.

In Michael's opinion, they were a perfect Army. A large enough group to do what was needed, but not so large as to draw unwanted attention as they rode. Valdez would lead one group and he the other.

"It is bold, Senor," Valdez told him, "to strike at them in two places at the same time. Do you wish the marshal killed in these raids?"

"If it is possible, yes," Michael told him. "Before long, we will bring such fear that the towns will not even be able to hire a marshal. Mainly, if you encounter any Rangers, kill all you can."

"But, Senor Michael, some of them are your own brothers."

"They were once," said Michael, "but not now. Now, you are my brother. You and Pedro. Kill all you have the opportunity to kill."

"What if we lose men ourselves?" Valdez asked him.

"Does any man ride with us who does not know it is possible?" Michael asked him.

"No," said Valdez, "they all have lived the bandit life for some years."

"Then, if someone is lost, we will replace them and continue. This includes you and me, too," he said.

Three days later, they left Chihuahua. Five rode toward Juarez and five toward Acuna. The ride they were taking would be a long one and Michael told them he hoped he would see them all back in Acuna in four months' time.

Michael rode with the group to Acuna and from there, they would ride to Houston. Valdez took his men north and they would stay that route until turning east and into Lubbock. In his time in Mexico, Michael had become fluent in their language. At night around their fires,

Michael was able to take part in the conversations. Somehow, it reminded him of better times back with his family before coming west. One of the men who rode with him was a brother to the woman Michael lived with in Chihuahua. He and Rosalina were not married by the church, but they were still considered to be by everyone in town and they thought well of him. The Mexican and the white man had been enemies since the first coming of the whites. As long as Michael kept his robbing and killing above the border, they would have no problem with him. One of his men asked how it can be that he has six brothers who were Rangers and he himself is a bandit.

"I have one brother, too," said Michael, "that is a man of God. A preacher in a grand church in Dallas. One day, maybe we will make a raid on his city too." He told them that as he grew up, his father had let all of his children make their own decisions. "I don't really know what made me different from them. Maybe it was that I kept seeing people who were in positions to help others abuse that position."

When they rode into Houston, it was not as a group. One rode in alone and the others as pairs and they rode in from different directions. This way, they drew less attention and also let them look the city over better. They met near the back of the stables and out of sight of the streets. Rosalina's brother, Pedro, told him he had seen two Rangers standing near the bank.

"There is sure to be a marshal somewhere around, too," said Michael. The Rangers would have to be killed first and fast before going into the bank. Those shots would bring the marshal from wherever he was.

"What if the Rangers are your brothers?" Pedro asked him.

"Then today, I will lose a brother," said Michael, "perhaps two."

"I do not want to kill your brothers," said Pedro. "You are my brother now and I would not want to kill you."

"Okay," he told Pedro, "you stay here and be ready to bring up the horses when we come out of the bank. Two will go in and two will kill the Rangers and the marshal when he shows up."

Michael and one of the others walked toward the bank, taking their time about it. They didn't want to seem eager in their movements. They stopped to look in the saloon door as they came to it, as if looking for someone, and then stood looking into the window of the general store. They were giving the others time needed to come up behind the Rangers. As he looked in the store window, Michael could see the bandits slipping up the alley across from them and right near the Rangers. They stepped out of the alley and called to the Rangers to turn and face their death. As they did so, Michael and his partner crossed the street and went toward the bank.

Before they reached the door, Michael saw that both Rangers were down and also one of the bandits.

They went through the door of the bank with guns drawn and quickly had everyone on the floor and the banker opening the safe at gunpoint. Michael heard two more shots from outside and hoped it had taken care of the marshal. The bank of Houston was heavy with paper money, but very little gold. That was fine with Michael, as gold was so heavy it slowed down their getting away. As they were leaving the bank, he told himself he would not look at the Rangers. He told himself he didn't care if it were any of his brothers or not.

As they went by the bodies, though, he couldn't help but look at the faces of the men laying on the ground. Neither of them did he know, but he did know the two bandits who lay dead. By that time Pedro was there with the horses and, in a cloud of dust and a few shots from some citizens, they were out of town, running their horses hard for the first mile or so, then slowing down.

Michael had lost two of his bandit friends in that one robbery. He would have to decide if it was worth even trying San Antonio with them now being shorthanded. He hoped Valdez fared better in Lubbock.

Valdez had, in fact, had even worse luck in Lubbock. He lost no men, but three had been wounded and their take had been very small. The bank had held almost no money in it. He hoped they would do better in Brownsville, even though it was a small town.

Isaac sat with Jacob in a small room in the main office of the Rangers headquarters in Austin. They were to meet with most of the Rangers in the next few days to try to put a plan into action. By now, all of the Rangers knew that the leader of this vicious band of thieves and murderers was led by the brother of six of their own brother officers. They hoped that the Blackstone brothers could, together, think what their brother may do next.

Rangers began to filter in as the day went on. Around one o'clock, a Ranger rode in with news that they had hit Houston. Two Rangers and the town marshal were dead and two bandits were dead as well. The Ranger who told this had not personally been there, so could not give a description of the dead bandits. It would have done no good anyway. Michael's looks had changed so much it was doubtful that his own brothers would know him if they passed him on the street.

At just after dark, three Rangers rode in together, having met up out on the trail. One of them had news that Lubbock had been attacked. That they knew of, no one on either side had lost men, but some had been wounded.

"Are they prisoners?" another Ranger asked.

"No, they were still able to ride and escaped with the others," he was told.

"Both of them happened today?" asked Isaac.

One Ranger produced the wire from his pocket. "According to this wire, they hit Lubbock about nine this morning. The report we got said it was around eleven thirty when they hit the bank in Houston and the Rangers were killed at the same time."

"How could they be in both places in the same day?" asked Jacob. "It is impossible. The two towns are days apart, even at a hard ride."

"Two different bands," said a Ranger.

"Two bands," said Isaac, "but with one leader, I believe. Michael split his group in two bands to throw us off."

"What makes you so sure?" asked the ranger who brought news of Houston.

"I'm not sure," said Isaac, "it was just a thought. None of us are sure of anything, are we? Until a few days ago we weren't even sure that these men were, indeed, led by my brother. When all of the towns that had been hit was written down, my youngest brother, Abraham, noticed that all but one of them was a town where we brothers had served as marshals at one time or another. At that time, he fought shy of them because of a promise we had all made to our father."

"What promise was that?" asked a Ranger.

"That we would draw no gun against each other," said Isaac.

"But he's an outlaw," said the same Ranger, "and you all are sworn peace officers. Not just town marshals now, but duly sworn to protect all of Texas. Do you still hold to that promise now?"

"Obviously, we can't do both," said Isaac. "That is one reason for this meeting, to decide if my brothers and myself should step down as Rangers."

"The decision is made," came a voice from behind them. They turned to find Leander McNelly standing there. McNelly was the leader of what was being called the special force, a large group of the newly reformed Texas Rangers. He and his Rangers were in charge of cleaning outlaws, bandits and rogue Indians out of central and south Texas. "Blackstone," he said to Isaac, "I can appreciate a promise made to one's father. Still, there are other ways for you and your brothers to contribute to the mission other than facing that bad seed brother of yours gun to gun. As you said, Abraham was the one who figured out for sure that it was, in fact, Michael we are after. From now until the close of this case, the six of you will gather information and between you, try to figure his moves until we can get ahead of him. That said, though, I nor any of these men, made such a promise to your father. Do we agree then, gentlemen?"

By the time the meeting was over, the next day all six of the Ranger brothers were there in Austin.

That same evening, Isaac called his brothers to a meeting of just themselves. They gathered in a small back room of the Austin Ranger headquarters building to talk and compare notes.

Just as they started, a Ranger came to the door, and said, "We just got a wire that Brownsville, up north, was hit late yesterday. The marshal and two citizens were killed. They got little more than pocket money."

When he had gone, Isaac said, "Okay, let's all make a list of what we know for sure. Then, we will all go over it and see if one knows something the others don't. First, I want to say, if you are not in this as a Ranger, leave now. I know the promise we all made to Pa, so if you don't want to take part in the capture or killing of Michael, you should leave now and no one will hold any hard feelings."

They all agreed to stay and help with all they could do. As Isaac and Josiah rode toward Abilene the next week for the first time since their father's death, they both thought it would be bittersweet if one of the bodies they were going to look at was, indeed, Michael's. To have been killed right where it all had started. This had all started two weeks earlier with a rash of stage holdups all around the Abilene area. They were described as a band of Mexicans, anywhere from four to eight of them at a time. The Rangers had quietly moved into the area themselves and at least two were riding inside all stages with routes near Abilene.

Four days into the operation, the bandits hit and, as it happened, there had been three Rangers on that trip. They caught them by surprise and cut the bandits to ribbons. When it was over, one Ranger had received a slight flesh wound to his arm and six bandits lay dead. As one of them rode a red horse, they notified the Blackstone brothers to come make an identification.

It was a long ride for the boys, not so much in miles, but in thoughts. Over the course of it, they both thought back to good memories of Michael, both here and back in Tennessee when they were growing up. When they arrived in Abilene, they went to the marshal's office. The Ranger there told them that two of the town's people had thought one of them was Michael, but they weren't certain.

"Well, let's go see," Isaac told him.

They went to the undertakers, and he took them in the back. As Isaac and Josiah moved down the line of bodies, they both had mixed feelings. They wanted it over, but not with Michael dead, even though both knew that would be the only way for it to end. One after the other, they looked at the bodies and, at the end of the line, they both shook their heads at the other Ranger.

"Michael is not there," they told him. "I can't say if they are his men or not, but he is not among them."

The Ranger looked at them and asked if they needed to look again.

"No," said Isaac. "From a distance, I may not know the man Michael is any longer, but up that close we would both know our brother."

"Write your report he is still out there somewhere."

Before leaving town, they visited with a few people they had known there. The next morning, though, they were on the trail back to Austin to let the others know.

When they reported to McNelly later, he told them, "That's okay. Sooner or later, we'll get him."

At that time, the Rangers had no way of knowing, but it would be later, much later. Back in Austin, they sat together and tried to figure what, if any plan, Michael had for his next hit. To date, the robberies that Michael and his band were blamed for, both in paper money and gold, came to almost a quarter of a million dollars. Of course, some of these may be like the ones just killed in Abilene and have nothing to do with him at all. Still, the gold taken in the San Angelo raid that was meant to be the Rangers' paydays was a major part of that total and could allow them to stop for a while at any time.

Little did they know, someone else who had just made it back to Acuna after a very hard ride, felt that same way. Michael would wait there for Valdez to arrive and then they would go to Chihuahua together. In the meantime, Michael got a bath and a shave and bought a change of clothes.

"It will be good to be back in Chihuahua and with Rosalina," he told Pedro.

"Yes," said Pedro, "it will be good to be home. This was a hard one, Senor, on all of us."

Two days after Michael and what was left of his men rode into Acuna, Valdez rode in from the north. He went to the cantina where they always met. Michael was there and stood as his friend approached.

"Valdez," he said, as they both sat, "it is good to see you, my friend."

"It is good to see you, too," he told Michael. "We had problems. I came in with three wounded men and very little else."

"You have fared better than I have," said Michael. "Houston was heavy with paper money, but at a price. I lost two men there and with that, I decided to not try San Antonio with just three men. What of you? Where were your men wounded?"

"In Lubbock," said Valdez. "The bank there held very little monies, and when we were leaving it, they were shooting at us from everywhere. We were lucky to get out at all. By the time we got to Brownsville, the wounded were a little better and we rode in on them. The bank there held little more and this time we were ready for them. The three who were wounded we left outside and, as we came out, they tried what Lubbock had done. As I say, though, this time we were ready and we left many dead there."

Michael and Valdez talked long into the night and both agreed it was time for them to lay low for a while. From Houston, they had a good amount of paper money.

It would be enough to hold them for a while. There was also still most all of the gold they had taken in their raids hidden away for just this purpose. For three months then, they made no forays into Texas.

Then, Michael called on the cousin who had spied for him before and sent him to Texas to see what he could find out.

A month later, he was back and came to Michael, and said, "They are gone, Senor."

"Gone?" said Michael. "What do you mean gone?"

"I see one here and there, but not like it was. When I asked a man there he say to me that McNelly's force is disbanded and sent all over Texas."

Michael would later learn that the special force Rangers were granted to McNelly for a year only and that year was over. Sure enough, the Rangers had been broken up and sent to other areas all over the state. In a way, this made things a lot better, not having a whole force of men out there concentrating on them alone. But it also now meant that he may run into one of his brothers in almost any town they went to in Texas. He asked Valdez to call the men together and said they would plan a raid.

For the first month, they hit only small towns and several times stages. The money wasn't much, but they ran into no Rangers or even town marshals. After their fourth raid, Valdez got him alone and asked to talk to him.

"What's up?" Michael asked him.

"It's the others," Valdez told him. "Well, all but Pedro. They wonder why we keep doing these little jobs. They grow tired of the small pay and a couple even wonder if it is because you are afraid you will meet up with your brothers."

"It's not that," Michael told him. "You know that, Valdez. I am waiting for information is all. I have ten spies all over Texas right now, watching and listening for what bank has the biggest cache of gold and cash. Two are supposed to be coming in tomorrow with what they have learned. You tell the men that, and that when I know where the money is, I won't care if God himself is guarding it."

Valdez told the men word for word what Michael had said and, when asked if he believed it, he said yes without question.

The next day, the spies came to see Michael one at a time. The first one he talked to had been up near Abilene and reported nothing much happening. The other one, though, had word that, in three weeks, a large shipment of gold would be in the Houston Bank. It was a large strike from somewhere in California and was headed East to New York City. It was reported to be over a million dollars in gold.

"This was not loose gold," he told Michael, "but already in bars."

Michael paid them both and sent for Valdez. They sat that night and planned the whole thing. They would need wagons, several of them. To haul that much gold, said Michael, at least three. Then, with those wagons being so slow they would need men enough to cover the trail behind them. Michael was far from stupid and he knew that the Rangers would surely be notified of this gold shipment. He figured there would be some in town and possibly even some riding with the gold. If it was his brothers, he was sorry, but this he could not pass on.

Eighteen men and three women, along with three wagons, left Chihuahua and headed for Houston the next morning. Three of the men rode along with the women to appear as couples. Among the women was Rosalina. When Michael told her his plan, she had insisted on being one of the women. The other two were the girlfriends of Valdez. Each wagon carried a load of different items to sell in Houston. That would be their cover. Who would suspect a nice Mexican couple selling pottery items or wood carvings to be involved in a bank robbery? Michael had an idea of going in the bank at night. He knew there would still be guards a plenty, but at least most of the armed citizens would be at home in bed.

He planned to be there at least two days before the robbery to just watch their routines about guard changes and the like. On the first of April 1877, the wagons rolled into Houston with three men on horseback. This was normal because there were still small bands of renegade Indians between Mexico and Houston. These men were protection for the wagons. Michael sat slouched in the back of one of the wagons, which had been parked at the edge of the alley across from the bank. He wore a large sombrero pulled down to cover his face, but so that he could still see the front door of the bank. Rosalina had clay pots and dishes on the tailgate of the wagon and occasionally sold a piece to a passing citizen.

The deputy himself came over and looked at the things. Or, perhaps he came only to look Rosalina over. If so, Michael could not fault him for it. She was a very beautiful woman, he thought. The other wagons were placed in likely places at other alley entrances.

The gold came in around ten a.m. of the second day. Twelve guards with shotguns rode in with it and stood about as the gold was carried into the bank. Before it was all in, four Rangers rode into town from the north and went to the marshal's office. Michael knew two of them for brothers, though it made no difference. When they walked into the marshal's office, Michael was glad them boys had been born in a barn, for the front door was left standing wide open. He also knew that the Mexican propped up sleeping against the porch post with his sombrero pulled down, was far from asleep.

That night, two of the Rangers, a deputy and an armed citizen stood guard. As the banker arrived to open up the next morning, he was accompanied by the other two Rangers, the marshal and a citizen to change the guard for the day. He'd not gotten a good look at the guards who spent the night, but he clearly saw these as they faced away from the door as the bank owner unlocked the door. The Ranger was David, so that meant Daniel had spent the night. He had grown up with those two and knew they would not be far apart. At times growing up, he'd heard them finish one another's sentences. They wcrc that close.

Michael slipped away from the wagon after they had gone inside and went to the stables. His own big red stood there, but he would not take him, not now anyway. The boys would know him for sure. He rode slowly away from town toward the west until the flash from up in the hills caught his eye. Turning, he rode right to them.

Valdez stood waiting as he rode in. "Michael, my friend, it is good to see you."

"You, too, Val," said Michael. Quickly, he told Valdez everything. Four guards at night and four during the day. Yes, two of the Rangers there were his brothers, he told Valdez, but it mattered not. Pulling a sheet of paper from his pocket, Michael showed him where to position his men on rooftops and alleyways and they could prevent any help from reaching the bank once the alarm was raised. He explained how he'd had the three horsemen who had rode in with them, sneak a rather large flat rock to the bank roof.

"I do not understand this," said Valdez.

Michael explained how placing it on top of the dynamite would force more of the explosion down on the roof, causing more concussion inside the bank.

"You are the smart one, Michael," said Valdez. "When do we go?"

"Tonight," Michael said. "We don't know when the train will be in to get it. Maybe even tomorrow. The guards change shift at six when the banker is leaving for the night. We will give them until eight to get settled in and we'll blast the roof. I only hope the blast knocks them over long enough for us to reach the floor. Start filtering your men into town about six. Remember, after we have left in the wagons, make a big show of things before pulling out. If possible, we want them to think their gold left there on your horses. As soon as you can, ditch or kill any who pursue you and come join the wagons."

When he got back to town, Michael told Rosalina to tell the other girls at five start taking what was left on their wagons down the alley and hide it. He also showed her on one wheel how he wanted the sacking wrapped around the wheels.

"Why do we do this?" she asked. "

It will stop the wheels from cutting so deep and showing the true weight of the wagons," he told her. "Will you show the others, please? It may not work, but with a little luck, maybe they will not suspect the wagons anyway until it is too late."

"Of course," she said, "anything for you, Michael."

He left her to go and find the riders and other men from the wagons to tell them it was to be tonight. By the changing of the guards at six, Michael had everything ready. He had told Rosalina, as soon as they heard the explosion, to bring the wagons around behind the bank. At ten until eight that night, Michael and four others climbed onto the roof of the bank without a sound. The sixth man was on another mission. The dynamite was in place with the large rock on top of it.

He and two of the bandits would make the ten foot drop to the floor, the other two had their ropes tied off and ready. Looking around town, Michael saw flashes from several of the positions of Valdez's men.

"Light the fuse and stand back," he told Pedro, "but be ready to go in right away."

Pedro lit the fuse and they ducked back to the building's edge and waited. With a horrendous explosion, a ten foot hole opened in the roof of the bank. Michael, Pedro and one other dropped to the floor below. All the place was filled with the acrid smoke and the dust of the building materials. As the last two came down the rope, a shot rang out and a bandit let go his rope and fell. Michael had seen the flash and put two slugs in that area. He didn't know if he had hit anything or not. The guards started firing from three different spots. They returned fire and knew they got at least one and maybe a second. It was still smoky and dusty as Michael eased his way along the floor. He came to a body, but couldn't see if it was one of theirs or his man. Rolling him part way over, Michael felt for the man's chest and found no badge there. He knew for sure one of his men was dead then. Probably the man who fell from the rope.

Michael reached the wall and stood up. He was easing along the wall when a voice said, "Tom, Tom is that you?"

In a muffled voice, Michael answered, "Yeah, it's me."

"Can you see anything?" the man asked him.

Dropping to the floor, Michael said, "No. You can't either," and pulled the trigger three times. As the other man hit the floor, bullets cut the air over Michael's head. Some probably from his own men because nobody knew where anybody else was.

The air was clearing through the hole in the roof. As it did so, one of the bandits spotted a glint from a badge. The Ranger who wore it thought himself hidden in the bad light, but as it cleared, he wasn't. The bandit made sure he paid for that mistake. In Spanish, Michael called to each of his men and got a response from all but one.

"I think we only have two more," said Michael. "Fan out."

Just as they started to move, Michael heard the back door being opened. As he drew on the figure standing before the open door, two shots roared and the man fell backward. Michael eased to the door and spoke before looking out. When he did so, he saw Rosalina with that .38 Derringer of hers pointed his way.

"You got him, girl," Michael told her, and went back inside. Looking down, he saw that it was the deputy. Where the hell was that other Ranger, he wondered? As he figured, the gold was locked in the safe.

"What now?" asked Pedro.

"Go open the front door," he told Pedro. "Be careful, though, there is still a Ranger in here somewhere."

"He is buried under the roof," said Pedro. "I find him myself. If he is not dead, he is badly hurt."

As Pedro did as he was told, the bank president tumbled in, followed by the sixth bandit and the banker's wife.

"Open it," Michael told him.

"I won't do it," said the banker. "You'll just have to kill me."

"We will," said Michael, "but not before you first watch her die slowly and painfully."

"You wouldn't dare kill a woman," he told Michael.

"You're right," he told him. "I wouldn't, but he will," said Michael, pointing at a bandit with at least six knives strapped on him. "He'll do it and do it slowly."

As the big Mexican started toward the banker's wife, he said, "Alright, alright, just don't hurt her, please."

Michael took the banker to the safe and stood, waiting. He heard occasional shots from out front, so the others were trying to get past Valdez and his men. He knew each man out there and knew that wasn't going to happen. The only other approach was from the rear and, after what he'd just seen, if they tried, Rosalina they would find it worse than the bandits out front.

When the door swung open, he stood there for a second just looking at that gold shine. Taking the banker back up front, he had Pedro tie both him and his wife up and put them in the banker's small, private office. He went to the back door, and opening it, he told the girls to come inside. Leaving one of the men at the back door, Michael led Pedro and the other two, followed by the women to the safe. Their eyes grew big at the sight of the shining gold bars.

"Carry what you can, but move as fast as you can and let's get it on the wagons," said Michael.

They all set about carrying the gold out. They soon had about all one wagon could haul and started on the next one. Every time he went out the door, Michael could hear sporadic shots coming from out front.

"Valdez is doing his job," he said to Pedro. When the other wagons were loaded, the women climbed aboard. The bandit killed climbing down the rope had been one of the wagon drivers. He would have to be replaced by one of the other riders.

Michael and Pedro made a last trip through the bank. Stepping into the office, Michael told the banker and his wife that someone would be along later to free them.

"You're not going to kill us?" he asked.

"No," said Michael, "we only wanted the gold." He then went to the wagon himself.

As they climbed up, Pedro told Michael, "Your brother, the Ranger, he was the one killed when the roof blew. I am glad for you that he is not the one you had to shoot."

"Dead is dead," he told Pedro. Even as he said it, he knew that none of them had ever checked the body. Perhaps Daniel was only injured and trapped under the wreckage. Michael told himself he didn't care and went on.

They left Houston headed west toward San Antonio. They went right down the road as if they hauled nothing more than the loads they had brought with them. For several miles in the early morning stillness, they could still hear gunfire from Houston. Valdez would give them another half hour then they would mount up and storm the streets, shooting and yelling as they rode out of town.

Twenty minutes later, Michael had them all pull the wagons up under some trees and, while the women fixed something to eat, they cut the wrapping from the wagon wheels and threw them in the fire. As they sat over their breakfast, back in Houston, Valdez ordered his men to their horses. As yet he had lost no men, but could account for at least three of the ones who had tried to go to the aide of the bank. One he knew for sure was the marshal. That badge was what Valdez had sighted on as he pulled the trigger.

Suddenly, from alley ways in all directions they came tearing through town, shooting at any and everything that moved and shooting the windows out of storefronts. Both Rangers came from a doorway, firing at the fleeing bandits, and were left lying in the dusty street as they raced north out of town.

David Blackstone looked at the other Ranger lying close to him and saw that he was dead. He had been shot twice himself in the leg and the shoulder, but neither appeared to be that bad. He headed to the bank with Daniel, not the gold, on his mind. Men were beginning to come from all directions and head toward the bank. One of them was a teller at the bank and opened the front door for them. Inside, they stopped staring at the gaping hole above them and the light of morning beginning to show through it. David first saw the other Ranger and, rolling him, over saw that he was dead. He had been shot at least twice. Once in the head.

Just as he found the deputized citizen's body, someone called from the back that the deputy's body was there by the back door. The bandit killed coming down the rope was also found.

"Where the hell was Daniel then?" David thought. If this had been Michael's work, would he have taken Daniel as a prisoner. *"No, that was stupid,"* he thought. There was at least ten men in the bank, all yelling and talking, but he kept faintly hearing something and finally David shot through the hole in the roof and told them to shut up a minute. As things quieted down, he heard what he thought he had before. Tearing at the rubble pile, he yelled, "I need some help over here!"

It took almost half an hour to move enough to free Daniel. He was barely conscience when he was lifted from his entrapment. Two men carried him and David followed over to the doctor's office. The banker and his wife were freed. David asked one of the men who had carried Daniel over to send a wire to the Ranger headquarters in Austin and report what had taken place.

When the doctor was through with Daniel, he dressed David's wounds. David sat in a chair at his brother's bedside all night. In the morning, the doctor came in and checked him. He told David that his brother's breathing seemed better, but that he had taken quiet a lick to the head. The doctor thought that he would recover, though.

As he started out again, he told David to talk to him. "I can't really say for sure if he'll hear you or not. If he can, though, don't you think it'd be a comfort to him to know you're here and that he's safe? Before that, though, I'd advise you to get something to eat. I'll be here a while longer doing some papers. Go on now."

David went to the café and ordered some breakfast. While he was eating, the bank president came in and over to his table. "What are you doing?" he asked David.

"I'm about to have breakfast," he said. "Would you care to join me?"

"No," said the banker, "I mean about the gold and the robbery."

"I sent out wires," David told him, "and as soon as I can get some help here, we will go after them."

"But they'll be long gone by then," he told David. "You have to get a posse together now and go after them."

"Get a posse together?" asked David. "And do you want to be one of them?"

The banker looked at him and, hanging his head, said no.

"Can't say as I blame you," David told him. "That bunch has done killed two Rangers and wounded both me and my brother. They've also killed your marshal and his deputy and some citizens along with that. They are one mean bunch. We'll go when help gets here."

They rode along at what seemed a snail's pace and Michael was sure they would be overtaken at any time. Three days out of Houston, they met two Rangers headed in that direction. They flagged the wagons down and, although Michael and Pedro were both ready, all the Rangers did was ask them if they had seen any riders.

"It would be a sizeable group," one of them said.

They asked where they were coming from and Rosalina told them, in broken English, that they had left Houston four days earlier after selling all their goods and were headed home.

"You folks ride careful," they said, as they were riding away.

When they were well out of sight, Michael had them pull up to rest the horses under some trees.

"I thought we would have to kill them," said Pedro.

"I think the plan worked," said Michael, "at least for now. They were looking for a bunch of men on horses, not three empty wagons headed home after selling their wares. If they just don't notice how deep the wheels are cutting."

"It would be hard," said Pedro. "I looked for myself and the road is so hard packed we leave little trail."

"Good," said Michael, "that will help. It's just so slow with these wagons, it will take most of three weeks to get to San Antonio. I hope Valdez takes them for a long ride or he will lead them right to us as slow as we are moving."

Valdez was three days out of Houston and still he saw no sign of pursuit from anyone. He was unsure what he should do. "I am afraid," he told the others, "that if we do not slow down, they will not find our trail to follow."

"Maybe the gold was not so important to them," a man said.

"Gold is always important," said Valdez.

"Maybe we killed all the Rangers and marshals and they are scared to come after us," said another.

"They are not scared," said Valdez, "but you may be right about them sending for more Rangers. We had better send a rider out ahead to watch for any coming this way. I would hate to run right into a bunch of them without any warning."

That night in camp, Valdez wondered how far the wagons had gotten. They were loaded heavy, so he figured they would not make more than ten miles a day, if that.

As Michael and his little band sat around the fire that evening, they heard horses coming.

"I hope it's not Valdez already," he said. "We are still too close to Houston."

The lookout ran into camp, and said, "Rangers coming, at least seven of them."

Michael faded into the night like a ghost. If it was Rangers, he may be recognized. As he went past the horses, he caught up the big red and trailed him behind. He made his way up a steep little hill they were camped beneath and tied the red horse. Then, he found a likely spot where he could see into their camp and see the Rangers as they rode in. He sighted them with his rifle as they rode into the camp. Seeing the women in camp threw the Rangers off some. They were hoping they had come on a part of the bunch of bandits. Only Pedro and Rosalina replied to their questions. The others acted as though they spoke no English.

"Riders? No," said Pedro, "like we told the other Rangers we have seen, no one except them and now you." He repeated, too, what Rosalina had told the others, that they had left Houston four days ago after selling all they had and were headed home.

"Where is home?" a tall ranger with eyes like Michael's asked her.

"We live in a little village between Chihuahua and Juarez," she told him. "Do you know Mexico?"

"Not much" he told her. "You folks ever heard of Michael Blackstone?" he asked loudly.

Pedro spat into the fire, and said, "We have heard of him. He runs with a group of bandits. They have robbed our village many times. Has he robbed you, too?"

"Well, no, not me," said the Ranger, "but they have robbed the bank in Houston apparently the day after you all left. We're headed there now."

Again, Pedro spat and said, "I hope you catch him and hang them all."

"Well, we won't keep you folks up any longer. It looks like your wives are getting beds ready. I would advise to keep watch for them along the trail, though."

"We will," said Pedro, "and thank you, mister."

"Blackstone," he said. "My name is Isaac Blackstone, and them two over there are my brothers."

"You are not kin to that bandit?" asked Pedro, with anger in his voice.

"No," he said, "no kin. We just happen to have the same last name. We're plumb shamed by it ourselves," said the ranger.

Michael waited a good fifteen minutes after they had ridden out before he went back into camp. As he walked in, he started to clap his hands, and said, "I applaud you all. If you grow tired of the bandit life, I believe you could find work on the stages in New York. Never have I seen a more convincing bit of acting in my life. Pedro, the spitting, that was perfect."

"Thank you," said Pedro. "You know, three of them were your brothers."

"I thought so," he said. "I couldn't see that well from where I was, but I thought the build looked like Isaac."

"Si, that is the one who did the talking," said Pedro, "but he said two more of them were brothers as well. Only, he said they were no kin to you. In fact, he said they were ashamed to have the same name as you."

"Two in Houston and three just here, that leaves only one more out there somewhere," said Michael. "Hope I don't see him soon."

"You are a strange one," said Pedro. "You are my friend, but you are a strange one."

"Rosalina," he said, "are you ready for bed?"

"With a bandit like you?" she asked. Then, smiling, she said, "Always."

They would be three weeks in reaching San Antonio. He would cut shy of town and not take the wagons in.

They rode into Houston late in the evening and Isaac went straight to the doctor's office. Seeing a light at the jail, the others rode there. As they went in the door, David rose to meet his brothers and the other Rangers. "Isaac didn't come?" he asked Jacob.

"Yes, he went to the doctors first. How is Daniel doing?"

"He's doing well," said David. "Once he had regained consciousness, he started getting better pretty quick."

"Where was he hit?" asked Josiah.

"He wasn't," said David. "When the bank roof was blown in, he had been walking across the room and was caught under it."

Just then, Isaac came in the door and he and David shook hands. "I saw the doctor," he told them. "He said he was releasing Daniel tomorrow. Was it Michael?"

"If it was, I never saw him," said David. "Daniel was in the bank, but he would not have seen anyone. It took us half an hour to dig him out, he was so buried by the roof debris."

"Where were you?" Isaac asked him.

"In the hotel, just about to go to bed, when I heard the blast. I shoved my feet in my boots and grabbed my rifle as I went out the door."

"Where was the other Ranger?" Isaac asked.

"Same as me, he came from his room as I reached the stairs. The marshal met us at the door and told us the blast had come from the bank. We tried for hours to get to the bank, but no matter how we went, they were ready for us and drove us back. We thought once we were going to make it, but again, they let loose on us and that's when the marshal was killed. They caught us in a cross fire from the roofs of several buildings at once. Ranger

Sanders and myself were driven back inside the hotel lobby. It went on like that for most of the night," said David. "They would quit firing for so long at times we just knew they had pulled out, but as soon as we stepped out, they'd open up on us again. About dawn, there had been another lull and we were just figuring to try for the bank again when they came tearing through town like the fires of hell were at their heels. Shooting at anything that moved and shooting out store windows.

"I guess they were just hoping to get one of us. That was when Sanders and I had decided to try again. He was hit first and I was hit once. I rolled him over and saw that he was dead. Some citizens showed up and, as they helped me up and off the street, they came tearing back up through town and I was hit again and two citizens were killed. I counted twelve of them, so I figured they were working half at the bank and half keeping us held off."

"What about the banker, what did he say?"

"Just that a big Mexican came to his house, kicked in his front door and took him and his wife to the bank. There, another bandit told him to open the safe and he refused until they threatened to cut his wife up and then kill her if he didn't. He said after he opened the safe, they were tied up and locked in his office until we got there and freed them."

"Did he notice one of them speaking English better than the others?" asked Isaac.

"I thought of that," said David. "He said they all spoke the same broken English. I also asked him straight out if he thought any of them was a white man. He swears they were all Mexicans. So, if it was Michael's gang and he was there, he was on a roof somewhere. Maybe it wasn't him at all. We've had no report of anyone that even sounded like his gang in months now."

"I don't know," said Isaac, "but let's all get some sleep and we'll ride north in the morning to see if we can pick up any sign of them. We are sure they went north."

They left town in that direction. "Isaac," said David, "I have no idea if they kept on it or not. Eight days after the robbery, someone finally rode out to try and find what direction the bandits had went once they were out of town. After a few miles of scouting, they found some sign of them. It wasn't much, but after a week, Isaac, I was surprised that they had found anything."

"Someone should have followed them soon after they rode out," he said.

David was becoming angry with his brother's remarks about how the whole thing had been handled. "Isaac, when it was over, I had a wounded brother buried under a pile of rubble. I also had two dead Rangers, a town marshal and his deputy both dead and wounded and dead citizens. The people were in no hurry to go chasing the men who had done it off to God knows where. I also want to say that my badge reads the same as yours, Isaac, Texas Ranger. You are not in charge here, in fact, it was my and Daniel's detail, so if you wish to remain here and help, then keep a civil tongue in your mouth or ride out. This is not your private war against Michael. If it is, you have no business being a Ranger."

Everyone sat without speaking for a minute and Isaac finally said, "You're right, David, I was out of line. I apologize to you and the rest of you men as well."

"Accepted," said David, "now, let's get a clear direction on these men, whether it be Michael's gang or not."

Another ten miles and they found where the bandits had stopped.

"They stopped here and made coffee," said Isaac.

"They were in no hurry, it appears," said David. "Of course, no one was chasing them. If men had rode out right behind them, they would have died right here. They would never have expected the bandits to camp this close to town."

Everywhere there were horse tracks. One of the Rangers came up to David, and said, "I've worked out the prints of twelve different horses, but if your brother is among them, he is not on that big red horse of his. I've studied them tracks enough to know."

"Thank you," said David. "We will ride back to town for the night and get supplied for a long ride. At sunrise tomorrow, we will start after them and ride them down unless they cross the border, and that is a good distance from here and in the other direction than they now travel."

When they rode into town, Daniel was at the marshal's office. "Daniel," said Isaac, "Are you well enough to be up and about?" "

"I'm as well as I have time to be," he told Isaac. "We have outlaws to catch."

That evening, the brothers all went to have dinner together for the first time in quite a while. As they sat there, Isaac told Daniel, "Well, I finally riled your twin today."

"You did?" asked Daniel. "That took some doing, big brother."

"Well, it wasn't easy. I've never seen either of you riled up in your lives. Pa always said you two were the most levelheaded ones and that Michael was the worst hot head in the bunch."

Suddenly, Jacob spoke up and said, "I hope it's not Michael. I hope he is somewhere in Mexico or even already dead. I've just never been able to get comfortable chasing down my brother to kill him." Looking around the table at his brothers, he said, "Please don't lecture me on what he's done. I'm well aware of it and I'm not saying he doesn't deserve to hang or be shot, for that matter. I just hope it's not me that has to do it."

None of them said anything for a moment, then Isaac said, "I think we all feel the same way, little brother.

Michael has held true to the promise he made to Pa, same as we did. To never raise a gun at one another. He even fought shy years ago of any town where we were the law. I respect him for that, but nothing else."

The next morning as they rode out of Houston, some one hundred and ninety miles to the north, Valdez and the other bandits were riding into Waco. Before entering town, Valdez had told them all to watch their behavior until they were ready to ride out. "We need to stay here a while," he said, "or they will lose our trail all together."

"That's good, no?" asked one of the bandits.

"No, that is not good," Valdez said. "We must lead them around for a while to give Michael the time he and Pedro need to get across the border. If they lose our trail, they may head off in a direction that would lead them right to the wagons. Those wagons will be loaded heavy and they will be slow."

He had them break up into small groups and pairs. They went to different saloons in town also so as not to draw attention to themselves. Not yet anyway, but in a few days, they would draw a lot of it before leaving town. They wanted to be well remembered when those Rangers made it to Waco. Not knowing exactly how far behind those Rangers were after five days of resting all day and drinking all night, Val told them to be ready to ride tomorrow.

Early in the morning hours, gunfire could be heard from every direction in town it seemed. The livery stable was burned, the general store robbed and the owner shot. In hearing the trouble there, the marshal had went over and he was shot and killed as he walked up, not even knowing what was going on.

Two weeks had gone by since the robbery and still the wagons creaked along ever so slowly. By his estimation, they were still a week out of San Antonio. Michael thought about taking the red horse and riding on ahead, but he would not. It would leave them shorthanded should they run into any Rangers. He knew where most of his brothers and several other Rangers were about now, but there were a lot more of them in Texas than just the Blackstone brothers. He would have given anything to be a fly on the wall when Isaac had gotten to Houston. Him being second oldest, he had always bossed the other boys around and acted like they could do nothing right. He and Isaac had clashed most of his life because he would not take it from him.

A week later they arrived just outside of San Antonio, they made camp under a stand of trees and the women started something for them to eat.

"In the morning, two will go to town for some supplies," Michael told them. "Speak to no one if not necessary and draw no attention to yourselves."

That night as he and Rosalina lay in bed, he told her if all had gone as planned, Valdez should be joining them before they reached the border. He had no way of knowing that they had waited on the Rangers to keep them on the trail.

"What if he doesn't?" she asked.

"We will go to Acuna and await him there."

Valdez decided they would wait on the Rangers no more. If they were to be led away from the wagons, they would now have the trail. He and the men were halfway to San Angelo and would push on come morning. He knew because of the delay he would not reach Michael before the border now. It could not be helped, though, because of those lazy Rangers, he thought.

Come daylight, they were in the saddle again and it was beginning to wear on everyone's nerves. The men were becoming ill tempered with each other. Valdez broke it up some by telling them that, when they reached San Angelo, they would blow off some steam.

"When we leave there, it will be only a dash to the border then to Acuna to meet with Michael and to divide all that gold," he told them.

When they rode into town six days later, they were rearing to go.

Valdez had laid up a whole day and night before they got there. The Rangers were in Waco hearing the story of how the bandits had robbed and killed the store owner and killed the marshal, shooting him down in cold blood.

The thing was, those men had been around town for several days someone told him.

They didn't even seem to know each other, said several people. Then, that morning two days ago, they banded together and did this for no reason that could be explained. This time, the Rangers lost no time in searching out which way the bandits had gone.

"West," said Isaac, as they sat by the fire that night. "Why do you think they would head west? Ask yourself this, if you were a Mexican bandit and had just robbed the bank in Houston, wouldn't you head as due south toward home as was possible?"

They all agreed with that.

"Then, why," asked Isaac, "did they go north to Waco and now they go west instead of going south again?"

"It's like they're just wanting us to follow them," said Daniel.

"It's exactly like that," said Isaac. "Boys, I think we are being led on a wild goose chase. I wonder if this bunch even has the gold."

"If not, then where is it?" Jacob asked him. "It was surely taken. Wagon loads of it."

"Damn it," said Isaac. "Do you boys remember the wagons we saw before reaching Houston?"

"Yeah," they said, "with the couples headed home with their wagons empty."

"I think those wagons may not have been so empty," said Isaac. He explained to Daniel and David what they were talking about.

"David," said Daniel, "do you remember seeing those wagons sitting around town for a few days before the robbery?"

"Yeah," said Daniel. "It was couples and they were selling pottery and leather goods and the like."

"Boys, we have been had," Isaac said.

"Was Michael there?" somebody asked him.

"No," said Isaac, "I'm sure we would have recognized him and I looked at the horses myself."

"Other than the wagon stock, there was only one extra horse and it wasn't the red," said Jacob.

"To hell with riding west," said David. "I say, come morning, we head for the border and hope to cut them or maybe even the wagons off. Do we all agree?"

Michael awoke early and built up the fire. As the others began to wake up, he told them he wanted to eat quickly and get an early start.

"I think you are smelling Mexico," said Pedro. "You are ready to be home, no?"

"Maybe," said Michael. "I just know I feel jumpy for some reason and want to be moving."

By the time the sun was rising in the eastern sky, they were already moving out of camp. "We still have about two weeks to the border," he told Rosalina, as they rode along. "I'd sure hate to be stopped this close after all we have been through."

That morning when they got up, Valdez called them all to the fire, and said, "I think we should ride for the border now. We have led these Rangers around long enough and I am ready to go home."

Within an hour, they were in their saddles and headed south.

Around the breakfast fire, the Rangers talked of what would be the best trails to take.

"Are we hoping to catch the riders or the wagons?" asked Josiah.

"I'd rather catch those wagons," said David, "if we agree that's where the gold probably is."

"Well, we are too few to split up," said Isaac. "If we did and found either one, they would cut us down."

"I think you're right about that, said David. "I say let's just ride hard toward the border. There's a town not far across it called Acuna that they may be headed for. If we catch either one, I'll be happy, gold or no gold."

Eight days later, Valdez and his men reached the border where the trail led to Acuna. They saw no sign of wagon tracks and Michael had also said if they got there first, he would leave a sign.

"We are here before them," he said.

"How can we be sure?" someone asked him.

"Well, I see no wagon tracks and no sign that Michael would have left."

"Are we to wait for them?" the bandit asked. "Or ride back and look for them?"

"No," said Valdez, "we will not go look. I will wait with some men, but those who wish to, can ride into Acuna and wait there. It is no more than ten miles from here."

Six of them would ride in, but if all had not come into Acuna in two days, they would come back and the rest could go into town. Valdez meant to stay right where he was until Michael showed up. The bandits swapped up going to town for another eight days.

Valdez had stayed there near the border the whole time. By now, he was beginning to worry that something had gone wrong. Maybe the Rangers had not followed them after all and had, someway, found Michael and the wagons first. Then again, it could just be that a wagon had broken down or a dozen other things.

The morning of the ninth day, a lookout Valdez had sent back up the trail a few miles came charging toward them at a dead run. As he came into camp, he told Valdez he could see the wagons coming maybe ten or so miles away.

"That's great," said Valdez.

"Maybe not so great," said the lookout, pointing north. "There is also a large group of riders coming from there and they ride hard."

"How far away are they?" asked Valdez.

"I am thinking they will get here together," he said.

Just then, the men who had been in town the last two nights, rode in and Valdez quickly filled everyone in.

"Do you want to go out to meet them?" a bandit asked.

"Only if we have to in order to keep them from getting the wagons" said Valdez. "We are in Mexico and they cannot come here for fear of starting a war."

With him shouting orders, the bandits were soon in hiding with a field of fire toward where the Rangers would be coming from, but still with good cover and still on the Mexican side of the border. When this was done, he jumped on his horse and tore up the trail toward the wagons to let Michael and the others what was happening and to speed them along, if possible.

Michael saw him coming at them and recognized who it was.

"Hold your fire," he told the rest of them, "it is Valdez."

When he rode up beside the wagon, he shouted, "Michael! You must go faster! The Rangers, they come, too, and it will be close as to who reaches the border first."

All three drivers heard him and lashed and shouted at their horses. As they neared the trail to Acuna, they heard shots and shouts, and looking northward, they saw the Rangers bearing down on them. One after the other, the wagons turned onto the trail to Acuna at a dead run. They did not slow up either, but kept on toward town. As the Rangers neared the border, a dozen bandits put shots right in front of their horses and then stood up rifles ready.

"This is as far as you go, amigos!" Valdez said loudly. "If you try to cross the border, we will kill you all and leave you for the coyote's!"

"It's no good," said Isaac, "they will do what he said. I just wish we had caught on to what was happening and turned south one day earlier."

"We did all we could," said David.

They had, too. For the last nine days, they had ate and slept in the saddle. They stopped only long enough to water their horses and the way they were pushing them, that had not been often enough.

Isaac sheathed his rifle and raised his hands toward the sky. Calling out to Valdez, he said, "You have the winning hand this time, my friend, but you tell Michael his day is coming!"

"Tell who?" asked Valdez, and swung to his horse and rode away. The other bandits stood their ground for another hour to make sure the Rangers didn't try to come in anyway.

As they rode away toward Austin, Isaac said, "Did you all hear what he said about tell who? Like he didn't even know Michael?"

"Maybe he doesn't," said Jacob. "You know, Isaac, there are other bandits in Mexico. Maybe Michael had nothing to do with this robbery at all."

"I don't believe that," said Isaac. "No band of Mexican outlaws planned this robbery by themselves. I'd bet my life on that. I'd also bet my life that, behind that lead wagon, was a rider on a big red horse."

"I sure hate to report this in Austin," said David.

"It's just part of the job," said Daniel. "If they don't like what happened, they can have my badge."

Michael

When Valdez caught up, Michael asked him what had happened and where were the rest of the men.

"We only warned them to stop," he told Michael, "and they did, so we killed no one. The other boys stayed for a while to make sure they didn't change their minds. What about you, did you have trouble?"

"No, not any trouble. I had just forgotten how slow it is to travel by wagon. When my family first came to Texas it was from Tennessee, back east and, brother, in a wagon that was a trip, I'll tell you. I think if the women had not been along, we would have went mad. We will stay tonight in Acuna and head for Chihuahua tomorrow."

"Sounds good to me," said Valdez. "I've forgotten what a bed feels like myself. We will split the gold there."

"That is fine. We all have a little for now."

"What now?" Valdez asked him.

"I think I may quit," said Michael. "Don't you ever think of finding one good woman and settling down?" he asked Valdez.

"No," said Val. "I think about finding a lot of bad women and staying on the move, though."

In Chihuahua, Michael and Val figured the split of the gold. After all were paid off and disappeared, he and Val sat talking still. "Were you serious about quitting?" Val asked him.

"I think so," said Michael. "I think I will quit and ask Rosalina to marry me. The two of us can live a long time off of this amount of gold."

"You will get old and fat" Valdez told him, jokingly.

"That might not be so bad," said Michael, "at least the old part. What about you, Val? Will you leave it?"

"One day, perhaps," he said, "but I still have a few good raids left in me I think."

"Well, you know you will always be my brother," Michael told him. "And if you ever need anything, all you need to do is say the word."

That night at supper, Pedro told Michael he would not be going back out with them. "As it happens," said Michael, "I won't be going back out myself."

Pedro's and Rosalina's eye's swung to him. "But what will you do?" Pedro asked him.

"I'll stay here and marry your sister, if she'll have me," he said. Looking at her, he said, "Well, will you?"

"Yes, Michael," she said, "you know I will."

"What about you, Pedro, what are you going to do?"

"Lita's father has a small rancho near here and he grows too old to work it all."

"Do I know her?" Michael asked him.

Rosalina said, "She is the girl who rode the wagon with him."

"Well, good for you, Pedro. I didn't even know you were serious with anyone."

"I wasn't when we left here," he said, "but it was a long wagon ride."

With a handful of gold coins in the plate, the padre agreed to marry both couples at the same time. Valdez would come by to see him once in a while and they would talk and drink the night away and then he'd be gone again.

Then, about three years after Michael quit, the bandits rode in one day and Valdez was not among them. Michael went to them and asked, "Where is my brother, Valdez?"

"In Austin, a Ranger recognized him, and without even calling his name to warn him, he shot Val dead in the street. Three of us, though, we make sure he will do no one else that way."

"Was it my kin?" Michael asked.

"No, Senor Michael," said the bandit. "This Ranger was little more than a boy."

Valdez was gone and Michael wasn't sure how to feel about it. Should he be mad at Val for not quitting when he and Pedro had, or mad at himself for quitting and letting his friend go out without him? His Pa had held a strong belief that every man must choose his own path. *"Look at me,"* thought Michael, *"I was raised in a home of love where there was education taught and religion taught, but also free thinking, and this is the path I chose. It could just have easily been me shot down in the street."*

Michael and Rosalina lived well from the gold they had taken in Houston. They were not rich, but they wanted for nothing. Much of the gold they had taken in the earlier robberies was still hid out. Only he and Valdez knew where it was hidden and now Valdez was gone. If it came to needing it, Michael would go for it and split it with Pedro.

He and Lita were doing well with her father's rancho. Pedro had bought some good breeding horses and had plans to raise them and sell them in Texas. They would bring a better price there than in Mexico.

After the death of Valdez, the other bandits just seemed to drift away one or two at a time. Michael didn't know if they were still robbing or not. For four years after the Houston Bank robbery, Michael set no foot in Texas. He lived happily with Rosalina in Chihuahua.

Then, in May of 1881, shortly after he turned forty-one years old, Pedro came to him one day and asked if he would help push twenty horses to Fort Worth with him.

"I have them sold to the man who supplies the Army," he told Michael. "We will go straight there and back. You know me, my bandit days are over just like yours are."

Michael agreed to go with him if they could stop back by the old home of his parents just long enough for him to visit their graves once more. It was agreed and they were to leave the next day.

That night, Michael was awakened by a bad dream. He couldn't really remember it after he was awake, but something about it left a coldness on him. He went in and woke Rosalina to tell her where the other gold was hidden in the hills outside of Juarez.

"Michael, why do you tell me this now?" she asked.

"I don't know," he told her, "just in case something should happen when Pedro and I go north with the horses." He made her tell back to him the directions he had given her to find the gold. By now, she was getting nervous and she asked him not to go.

"I have to go," said Michael. "He is your brother and has been my friend for many years. I let Valdez ride away alone and he did not come back."

"That was not your fault," she said. "Valdez, he should have quit being a bandit like you and Pedro did and he would still be alive."

"You are right," he said, "but we are not bandits anymore. We are businessmen delivering horses, no more, no less."

As he started out the door, he kissed her and told her they would be back in less than three months.

"I love you, Michael, she told him. "Please be careful."

"I love you, too," he said, and went out the door. He saddled that big red horse of his. Of all the horses he'd ever ridden, this old work horse rode best of all. Especially on long rides.

At the rancho, Pedro was awaiting his arrival. As he brought the horses out of the gate, Michael admired them all. They were some fine looking horses and he told Pedro so as he rode through the gate and closed it behind him.

"Thanks, he said, "I still want to borrow that horse of yours one day. He would sire some good colts."

"No he wouldn't," said Michael. "He gave that up years ago to become a team horse."

"You mean, he is..."

"A gelding," said Michael, "but he thanks you for the offer."

Now, pushing horses and pushing cattle are nothing alike. Horses move faster, they don't try to stray as bad and they won't stampede at the drop of a hat. It was much easier on the cowboys. At dark the first day, they were both tired, though, just because they had ridden so little lately.

Over the fire, they talked of the long rides they used to make sometimes for almost nothing. "I could not do it now," said Pedro.

"I don't think I could either," Michael told him.

Everything went great, and twenty days after leaving Chihuahua, they rode in to Fort Worth. It had been years since they were last here.

Also, as both of them had aged and changed in appearance quiet a lot, they had no fear of being recognized. They found an empty corral for the horses and Pedro went to find the buyer while Michael watched over them. Pedro was soon back and had a man with him. He looked at the horses and, after a few minutes of dickering back and forth, they agreed on a price. They shook hands and the man asked Pedro if he could wait until the bank opened in the morning for his money.

Pedro looked over at Michael, who nodded okay, so he told the man they would stay the night. When he had gone, they walked their horses to the livery stable and then went to find something to eat. They had a good meal and then walked to the hotel for rooms. They paid the clerk and went upstairs. Pedro asked Michael if he wanted to go to the saloon for a drink.

"I think I'll pass," Michael told him, "but if you want, I have a bottle in my saddle bag."

So, they sat in Michael's room and had a few drinks. It didn't take them long to figure out that long riding wasn't the only thing they had lost a taste for. Pedro went to his room and Michael went to bed.

At eight in the morning, they went downstairs and over to the café for breakfast. When they finished eating, Michael went to the livery stable to saddle their horses while Pedro met the man at the bank. When Pedro arrived, they mounted up and rode out. They were well out of town before Pedro finally said anything. When he did, it wasn't what Michael wanted to hear.

"I think a Ranger who was in front of the bank recognized me," he said.

"Surely not," said Michael, "not after all this time. You have changed a lot my friend. Maybe you were just nervous."

"Maybe so," said Pedro, "but I didn't like it."

They pushed on for a good forty miles that day before making camp. Pedro wanted to get as far from Fort Worth as possible, he said. They sat long over the fire and talked of the raids and of Valdez and others who had rode with them.

"It will be good to see the old place again," Michael told him.

"You lived there many years?" asked Pedro.

"No," Michael told him, then went on to tell him how his Pa had foreseen the war coming and moved them out here from Tennessee. "Still, it was where we stopped and lived for a while and both my mother and father are buried there. I wouldn't mind living there myself," said Michael.

"Buy it," Pedro told him, "and you and Rosalina move there."

"No," said Michael, "I did far too many bad things there. The people around there will never forget me, I'm afraid. Besides, I have come to love Chihuahua and its people."

They were up early and in the saddle soon after. A week after they left Fort Worth, they were sitting on a little hill looking down at where the home place had been. There was now a town there. It wasn't a very big, but it was growing according to the work going on around it. They rode in and the first man they saw, they asked what is the name of this town.

"Sweet Water," he said.

"How long has it been here?" Michael asked him.

"Around three years," he said. "I've only been here a year myself, though."

Michael told him his name and asked if he knew where his parents graves could be found.

"Sure thing," he said, "the church at the other end of this street has a cemetery behind it."

They told him thanks and rode toward the church. Michael went to the door on the side of the church and knocked. It took several times, but at last, the door opened.

"The front doors are wide open, son," said the preacher. "You could have come in through there."

"I am not a fit person to enter by the front doors," Michael told him.

"Not fit?" he asked. "Son, we are all the children of God and all of his children are welcome in his house. Come in."

As he did so, Michael could see that this was in fact the preacher's private quarters. "I'll not keep you long, sir," said Michael. "I'm looking for some information about the graves of my mother and father. This was our home place many years ago and they were both buried here."

"You'd be a Blackstone then?" the preacher asked him.

"Yes, sir," said Michael, "I am one of them."

"Well," he said, "I know where the graves are. In fact, I'd like to tell you a story about them. You see, I used to be a traveling preacher. That's to say, I rode from town to town spreading God's word then moving on. I was headed west of here one day and my horse came up lame, so I stopped here for the night to let the leg rest. At that time, there was part of a cabin still standing over in that direction," he told Michael, pointing at where he meant. "As I said, my horse was lame, so I was stuck here over night. I went to the creek for water and, Mister, that was the best water I had ever tasted. The next morning, I walked around some and came upon the graves. They were long left untended, so I set about doing it myself. While I was down on my knees pulling weeds, a voice told me that this was where I was to stay. I did just that. I built my church first and then, when some people started to come here from Abilene to hear me preach, they asked what was the name of my town and I told them Sweet Water, and that's what it is. Come on, I'll walk you out to the graves."

As they walked, Michael told him that he appreciated what he had done for his parents. "It was nothing, son. I like to think someone back in Virginia will do the same for mine. Met a couple of your brothers about a year or two ago. You a Texas Ranger, too?"

"No, sir," he said, "I'm the one called Michael."

"I guess I've heard of you, too," he said.

"Now you know why I didn't come in through the front of the church."

"I said I have heard of you and what you have done,"
he told Michael. 'Those things you will have to answer to
God for one day, but in the meantime, you are still
welcome in his house, Michael."

It took him a minute to realize they had been stopped
for some time, and looking over, he saw the graves of his
ma and pa.

"I'll leave you now," he told Michael, "but please,
come back by the church before you leave, will you?"

"I will, sir," said Michael. He stood and talked to his
mother and father as though they were sitting right in
front of him. He apologized to them for being such a bad
son all those years and for bringing shame to Pa's name.
"I have no right to ask for your forgiveness, or God's, but
I know now that I was wrong. I have quit being a bandit
and have married a fine Mexican lady. We live in
Chihuahua and I am happy there with her."

A little longer he stayed, and then he told them he
would visit again when he could. He stopped back at the
church and told the preacher they must be going, but if it
was okay, he would visit again.

"You come back any time, Michael, you are always
welcome here."

He and Pedro mounted up and rode to the south.
"Let's go home," he said to Pedro.

When they were no more than a mile out of town, he
was suddenly knocked from his saddle. As Pedro

dropped from his horse, he could see that Michael was hit very hard.

"Come on, my friend," said Pedro, "we must get you away from here."

"I won't be leaving here, Pedro," said Michael/ "I am afraid you will have to go on alone this time."

They could hear a rider coming and he told Pedro to go.

"I won't leave you, Michael," he told him.

"Pedro, go. If it is a Ranger, he will kill you, too, my brother. Tell Rosalina I love her for me and I'll see you down the trail sometime, okay? I think I'll take a little nap. I feel so sleepy all of a sudden."

Pedro hit his saddle, and as he raced away, he heard the bullets whine over his head.

The young Ranger stood over Michael, and said, "I knew when I saw your friend back in Fort Worth, you wouldn't be far away. I killed that other murdering friend of yours thinking he was you. Then, those who rode with him made a similar mistake and killed another Ranger thinking he was me. But, by God, I got you this time," he said.

A flash of light caught his eye just as the bullet ripped through his chest very close to his badge. He fell backward into the dust and he was dead. Michael took one last breath and he was gone also. The preacher had heard the shots and asked another man to ride out there with him. It was the man who had sent Michael and Pedro to the preacher to start with. When they rode up, the preacher dropped from his horse and, seeing who it was, he checked them both for life but there was none. He asked the other man to go back for a wagon to carry the bodies into town. He would go to Abilene tomorrow to wire Michael's brothers to see what they wanted done with the bodies.

Pedro could hardly see to ride for the tears in his eyes. Michael had been his best friend for so long and his brother-in-law for years. He dreaded telling his sister of Michael's death, knowing how much she loved him. The whole town did, for that matter. Here, in Texas, he may have been known as a bad man, but in Mexico, he had been a hero to many both young and old. It would be a long ride home, but he had heard Michael's gun as he fled and knew that the Ranger was gone, too.

The wire was sent to the Rangers Headquarters in Austin. It said that the outlaw Michael Blackstone and a young Ranger had killed each other just south of Sweet Water and asked to please advise what to do with the bodies. He stayed in Abilene the rest of the day to await a return wire. It was nearly six that evening when it came.

"Please take them to Abilene and we will arrive as soon as possible." It was signed, Isaac Blackstone.

Isaac, Daniel and David had been working from the headquarters for the last two years and, even as the preacher was reading the wire from him, he was telling them about Michael's death. They sent wires to Jacob and Josiah in San Angelo and Abraham in Fort Worth. The last wire was to Samuel in Dallas. Five days later, they were getting off the train in Abilene.

They went directly to the undertaker and told him who they were.

"I know," he said, "I remember you from when you was the marshal here, Isaac."

They were led to an icehouse in the back and first they viewed the body of the Ranger. Isaac told the undertaker his name and that he knew of no family the boy had. He also wasn't sure when he was born.

"Just do a standard service and funeral and send the bill to headquarters," Isaac told him.

"Very well," he said, and opened the wooden box beside it.

As they looked, they all knew it was Michael. He was heavier and much darker of complexion. There was some graying of his dark hair at the temples, but it was Michael.

As the brothers were having breakfast the next morning, a man approached their table. "Gentlemen," he said, "my name is Reverend Clarence Upton. I am the one who sent you the wire about your brother."

Isaac stood, and said, "Reverend Upton, would you join us, please?"

"Thank you," he said, sitting down. "I have met a couple of you, but it was some years back now and I'm not sure which ones it was."

Samuel spoke up and said, "Reverend, I am Samuel, the oldest of the brothers." Then, pointing to them he told the reverend who each one was and where he fit in line.

When he had told who Abraham was and that he was the youngest, Reverend Upton said, "I believe you forgot one, Samuel."

"No, sir, I don't think so," he said.

"What about Michael?" Upton asked him.

"Well, I haven't included him in listing my brothers in a number of years, Reverend Upton."

"But, when I spoke with him shortly before he was murdered, he told me all of your names and ages. He told me you were a pastor in Dallas and that the rest of you were Texas Rangers."

"What do you mean just before he died?" asked Samuel.

"Just that," said Reverend Upton. "He came to visit your parents' graves and we talked for quite some time. Anyway, I talked to the undertaker and he has told me that you all intend to bury Michael on Boot Hill here in Abilene. Is that correct?"

"That is what we were thinking," said Isaac.

"May I ask you why?" he said to Isaac.

"It's just the way things are done if you live and die by the gun," Isaac told him.

"So, then, the young Ranger will be buried there as well?" asked Upton.

"No, sir," said Isaac, "he will be buried in the church cemetery."

"I do not understand," said Reverend Upton. "The Ranger lived and died by the gun just as your brother did."

"I beg to differ," said Isaac. "Michael was a thief and a murderer. The boy was a man of the law."

"A man of the law who waited in hiding until your brother left my town and then, without any warning, shot him from cover. Even in death, you try to judge him and not leave that to God. When did you plan to bury him?" Upton asked.

"Today," said Samuel. "We all have other things to do and need to get back to them."

"Did you write to his wife in Chihuahua and tell her it would be today so that she may come?" he asked Samuel.

"I know of no wife in Mexico," said Samuel. "Possibly some whore he was living with."

"No," said Reverend Upton, "no, they were married in church by a minister of God; he told me that himself."

"What exactly is it that you want, Reverend Upton?" Isaac asked him.

"I wish to take Michael back to Sweet Water and bury him there beside his father and mother, who right now, I believe, were the only people in his younger life that truly loved him."

"I absolutely will not agree to that," said Samuel. "He was a great embarrassment to my parents for years."

"I don't believe that," said Upton. "I think he was to you as a pastor and to the rest of you as Texas Rangers, but I do not believe he was to his parents."

"May we talk among ourselves and let you know?" asked Isaac.

"I will await your decision at the general store," he told them.

After he had gone out, Isaac said, "I wonder why his interest in Michael?"

They all agreed that they couldn't figure what difference it would make to a stranger where Michael was buried.

"I guess," said Samuel, "in really looking at it do, we have a right not to bury him beside Ma and Pa. I mean, I was uncomfortable with it myself, but I intend to be laid to rest there myself one day. Because of the life he led makes Michael no less Ma and Pa's child than we are. I say we let the Reverend Upton bury him there if he wants to," said Samuel. "Do we agree?" he asked.

As when they were kids, six arms raised and lowered, and Isaac said, "If you all would like, I'll go tell Upton."

They all nodded and he rose from the table. As he entered the general store, Reverend Upton turned around to face him. "Well, have you and your brothers made your decision?" he asked.

"We have," said Isaac, "and if you wish to bury Michael beside our parents, it is okay with us."

"Thank you," he told Isaac, "and tell your brothers for me, too."

"May I ask you something?" Isaac said.

"Certainly," said the reverend.

"Why is it so important to you where Michael is buried?"

"I don't know really," he said. "He just seemed so lonely for family when we talked. He could have told me he was any one of you and I would have known no difference. He didn't, though. He told me who he was and also what he was. Then, at the graves, I saw a genuine love for his parents in him. Did you know he has not been out of Mexico in the last four years?"

"No," said Isaac, "but I'm sure he has been blamed for things he never done in that time."

"He had no reason to lie to me," said Upton, "for I judged him not. I will not wait his burial for them, but I will contact his widow and her brother who was with him that day to come and visit his grave."

"I think that would be the right thing," said Isaac. "I am glad that Michael met you."

"Well, I'm glad I met him, too," Reverend Upton said.

The next day, the body of Michael Blackstone was laid to rest beside his mother and father in that little cemetery in Sweet Water, Texas.

In time, Rosalina and Pedro did make the trip to visit it and to visit with the preacher as well. Michael's brothers did not stay or attend his funeral. They never came again that he knew of, but they did have a headstone carved and sent there to go on his grave. It read simply, "Michael Blackstone, born 1840 died 1881. Beloved husband and brother."

The End

POEM

"8"

Ma and Pa had eight tall sons,

And all of them went west.

Each of them could use a gun,

But one was always best.

One of them turned to the lord,

And six upheld the law.

The other practiced every day,

To be the fastest draw.

Each of them tried pointing out,

The road that he went down.

He told them all to go to hell,

And headed out of town.

For years they saw the posters,

And heard the things he'd done.

But they would not go after him,

He was still their father's son.

One day his luck came to an end,

Or so the paper read.

After years of doing evil deeds,

That he at last was dead.

Some whispered that it was his gang,

When the town filled up with strangers.

Then they learned one was a priest,

And the rest were Texas Rangers.

Lightning streaked the morning sky,

With a boom of cannon thunder.

Skies were gray with falling rain,

The day they put him under.

Seven men stood round the grave,

Upon the cold. wet sod.

Six of them wore silver stars,

And one a man of God.

No wife or children gathered there,

Nor friends that could be found.

That's how it very often was,

When an outlaw went to ground.

The priest finished with his prayer,

And turned and walked away.

The rangers stood a moment more,

But without respects to pay.

When at the bottom of Boot Hill,

They stood and faced each other.

Glad the outlaw's life was done,

But sad to lose their brother.

www.ingramcontent.com/pod-product-compliance
Lightning Source LLC
Chambersburg PA
CBHW071441130726
47997CB00006B/2185